T0273597

THE LAWS OF THE SKIES

Grégoire Courtois

TRANSLATED *by* RHONDA MULLINS

COACH HOUSE BOOKS | TORONTO

First English-language edition. Originally published as *Les lois du ciel* by Le Quartanier, 2016.

 CENTRE NATIONAL DU LIVRE

Coach House Books gratefully acknowledges the financial support of the Centre national du livre, an initiative of the Ministry of Culture of France. Thanks, also, to the Government of Canada through the Canada Book Fund.

LIBRARY AND ARCHIVES CANADA CATALOGUING IN PUBLICATION

Title: The laws of the skies / by Grégoire Courtois ; translated by Rhonda Mullins.
Other titles: Lois du ciel. English.
Names: Courtois, Grégoire, author. | Mullins, Rhonda, 1966- translator.
Description: Translation of: Les lois du ciel.
Identifiers: Canadiana (print) 20190061367 | Canadiana (ebook) 20190061383 | ISBN 9781552453872 (softcover) | ISBN 9781770565951 (EPUB) | ISBN 9781770565968 (PDF)
Classification: LCC PQ2703.O97 L6513 2019 | DDC 843/.92—dc23

The Laws of the Skies is available as an ebook: ISBN 978 1 77056 595 1 (EPUB), ISBN 978 1 77056 596 8 (PDF).

Purchase of the print version of this book entitles you to a free digital copy. To claim your ebook of this title, please email sales@chbooks.com with proof of purchase. (Coach House Books reserves the right to terminate the free digital download offer at any time.)

I

The moms and dads had said goodbye to them through the school bus windows. Some of the children were crying as they waved goodbye, and others were chattering with each other as if they had never had parents. It was the first time any of them would be away from their home, their bed, and their blankie. Some of the parents were emotional; sending such young children away from their families, they thought, even well supervised, even just a handful of kilometres from home, was a big risk, maybe even traumatizing. But worried though they were, the parents weren't going to go so far as to keep their children home from camp, weren't going to let the others go while keeping their own precious offspring safe and sound, afraid they would miss out on memories and experiences that the group was going to have and would show off like shiny jewels.

So they all left, the twelve children from the Grade 1 class of the Claincy primary school in Yonne, accompanied by their teacher, Frédéric Brun, whom all the children called Fred; Sandra Rémy, Jade Rémy's mother; and Nathalie Amselle, Hugo Amselle's mother.

The bus pulled away along the village road, and the parents' long shadows shrunk behind the condensation-covered windows.

And there you have it.

The children were on their way.

They would never return.

The lightly wooded plains to the south of Yonne start to blister and crack as you approach the Morvan mountain range. The carpet of green is dotted with taller and taller trees, and small rocks grow larger and larger until they split the earth and lift the ground. Very soon, as you continue south past Vézelay, the landscape becomes a curtain of tall trees and chaotic topography that strangle contour lines. In the undergrowth running alongside the bus's route, you can detect the presence of more and more wild animals – deer, foxes, buzzards – but the unruly, excited, noisy children were not concerned by them, had not listened to Fred's insightful explanations, and kept laughing, talking, singing, kicking each other under the seats.

'Frédéric, I don't know how you don't have a headache every night when you get home,' Sandra Rémy said.

'They're excited about the trip,' the teacher said. 'They're not always this rowdy.'

He smiled, but his smile appeared frozen in worry rather than natural when he looked at Nathalie Amselle.

'Are you okay, Nathalie?' he asked.

'I'm okay,' Nathalie said. 'My stomach is just a bit upset. Something I ate didn't agree with me, I guess.'

Sandra Rémy saw the look exchanged between Nathalie and Frédéric, and in the space of an instant, the furtive thought crossed her mind that there might be something between the two of them, something beyond the cordial relationship expected between parents and teachers. Was she the foil for a class trip whose sole purpose was to indulge the desires of lovers having an extramarital affair? The mere shadow of this idea made her slump scowling in her seat, hoping her hunch would be quickly proven wrong.

'I'm going to park over there, on the shoulder,' the driver said. 'The dirt road is just a hundred metres away, and if I head down it, we might get stuck in the mud.

'Okay,' Fred said, putting on his backpack.

Then, turning, he said, 'Okay, kids, this is it! I want you to put all your trash in the trash bags, and don't forget anything. Another bus will be picking us up, so take a good look around.'

The bus stopped, and the children's clamour filled up the space, a terrible racket that went straight through the head of Sandra Rémy, who, wide-eyed, was horrified at the idea that the trip had just started and already she had the burning desire to scream and hit any one of the crazed little demons.

A few minutes later, the bus was pulling away in a nauseating cloud of thick smoke, and the little group, backpacks on, was headed to the dirt road that led into the forest.

'Look carefully around you, children,' Fred shouted, 'and tell us if you recognize a plant or an animal that we studied in class, okay?'

The instructions made the somewhat ordered ranks of the fragile procession fall out, and the children started amusing themselves in uneven clumps on either side of the road. The walk was seriously slowed: the children were crouching and kneeling, some were even lying on the ground to observe moss, lichen, dead wood, beetles, and slugs, in a noisy assortment of exclamations, invectives, and vague questions for the teacher, although none of them listened to the answers.

'What happens when you crush a snail?' Enzo asked Lilou.

She stared at him, eyes wide with terror, before turning to look at his raised foot, which was threatening to come crashing down on a little snail's bright yellow shell. Enzo was sporting his usual smile, and it was hard to tell whether it was the smile of a deranged child or a deliriously happy one. Regardless, anyone who met Enzo found him to be a creepy little boy, even if it was just an unpleasant sense of foreboding. The violence that came through in everything he did and everything he said made him a danger to be avoided. In his presence, people got in touch with their primitive survival instincts. Without realizing it, they tried to avoid him, and when they found themselves stuck with him, they feared the situation could degenerate at any moment. Little Lilou had that very feeling when Enzo slowly lowered his foot onto the snail, in silence, so that the sinister crack of the shell being crushed could be heard loud and clear. An irrepressible sob rose in her throat.

'A crushed snail is just a slug!' Enzo yelled, laughing like a boy unhinged.

And he took off running, zigzagging through the tree trunks on the carpet of rotting leaves. Lilou swallowed her saliva, came back to her senses as if waking from a dream, and looked around her. A few metres away, Sandra, Jade's mom, was petrified. She had seen what had happened without daring to intervene. Lilou knit her brow, her eyes dark and lightly veiled with tears, and ran toward a group of friends. Enzo's laugh echoed through the undergrowth.

Nathan, Louis, and Océane were the best friends in the world. They did everything together, gathered together every day at recess and would have liked to sit together in class, if Fred hadn't separated them because of their endless chatter. On weekends, they went over to each other's houses and sometimes even managed to talk their parents into letting them spend a few days of vacation together. None of them knew it was love, but clearly Nathan loved Océane, Océane loved Louis, and Louis loved his two friends with pure, unshakable devotion.

Today, as was their habit, they wandered away from the other students, carried off in a fantasy of their making, entering the woods by diving stealthily from thicket to thicket, from holly bush to bright bramble patch. Océane was hunting forest trolls. She was commanding the elements, making the treetops bow, rendering water potable, and conjuring flames with just her voice. Nathan was her faithful assistant, whose duties consisted of carrying her things and collecting ingredients for his mistress's spells and potions. As for Louis, he was pretending to be a mysterious wild man, half human, half wolf, whom the enchantress had just met and who offered to guide her to the trolls' secret lair. The three friends blazed a trail through the trees and seemed to be heading into the depths of the dense, fabulous forest, but, in fact, the children's path was merely tracing a line parallel with the dirt road, their fear and diligent obedience ensuring that they never lost sight of it.

'What was that sound?' Nathan asked.

Louis tried to offer a fantastic explanation in keeping with his role as a wolf man, but he was somewhat worried and settled for shrugging his shoulders. The three children looked at each other in silence, and Océane winked before setting off at a brisk pace in the direction of the mysterious sound. Caught off guard, the two boys had no choice but to trot shamefully behind her. A few metres later, they discovered their friend lying on her belly near the trunk of an ash, her face contorted, wide-eyed, staring at a pale shape raising its flaccid roundness some fifty centimetres above the ground. There was no doubt that this was where the awful noise, and other more disgusting things, was coming from, producing a thundering roar, a thick gurgling punctuated by muffled explosions, the echo of which rebounded off the bark of the trees.

You would have to have no sense of sight, sound, or smell not to realize that Nathalie Amselle was truly sick, and the stunned children faced with this excremental scene realized it in the most shocking of ways, cheek to cheek with the rosy posterior of a woman who seemed to contain more poop than the septic tank they sometimes spotted when peering down the hole of the old-fashioned squat toilets in the aging recreation centre buildings. Unaware that three little sets of eyes were staring at her backside, Nathalie was crouched and moaning, contorting herself to expel the ochre pulp from her body, finally collapsing onto her hands and knees to vomit whatever lingered in her stomach. Her soiled bum exposed, bile dripping down her chin, her eyes met those of the children and, although a wave of shame initially washed over her, the compassionate, concerned, understanding looks of the three friends prevented her from feeling too pathetic.

'Are you sick, ma'am? Do you want me to get Fred?' Océane offered.

'Oh, no. Please don't! No, thank you, children,' Nathalie replied, wiping her bum with a handful of dead leaves. 'I'll be fine. Go back and join the others and don't stray too far from the path.'

The enchantress, her assistant, and the wolf man nodded, and the three set off running in the direction of their class-mates' cries and laughter.

'Fred! Enzo kicked me!'

Yasmine was holding her knee, aping intense pain, and limping along the dirt road, leaning on her friend Emma.

'Enzo!' Fred yelled. 'Come here!'

'I'm right here,' said a flat voice behind him, making Fred jump in surprise and, without wanting to admit it, a bit in fear as well, realizing that this child seemed to have the power to appear behind his victims and maybe even disappear just as quickly if threatened or cornered. He had never known how to talk to Enzo or how to make him understand the basic rules of life in society. Every explanation and admonition slid off him like water off sheet metal: smooth, cold, insensitive, sharp. And yet, out of habit or because he had exhausted every other pedagogical approach in his arsenal, Fred continued to scold Enzo when he caught him doing something wrong. His words fell on deaf ears, but at least the other students would see that no one was above the rules. This was the absurd song and dance that had just started.

'Why did you kick Yasmine?' Fred asked.

'Because she was in my way,' Enzo replied.

'And you couldn't just talk to her about it?'

'There's no point talking to some people. You have to smack them. It's the only thing they understand.'

Fred stared wide-eyed. 'That's not the least bit true! Who told you that?'

'My dad,' Enzo replied coldly, 'and he knows what he's talking about.'

'Well, I don't agree with your father,' Fred sputtered, 'and I'll tell him so when I see him. There is always room for discussion. There is no need to resort to violence.'

'But you want to hit me right now. Why don't you hit me?'

Fred was slack-jawed for a moment. 'No I don't. I have never wanted to use violence, not with adults and particularly not with children. There is always a way to –'

Enzo lifted his hand solemnly, shutting Fred up. 'Then you're weak. That's what my dad says, and he's right. Strong people hit; weak people get hit.'

The child's scowl pierced Fred's heart like a poison arrow. At just six years and a few months, this puny little being embodied the impotence the teacher sometimes felt.

'You should hit me if you feel like it,' Enzo said.

Watching this frosty duel, Yasmine had completely forgotten her pain.

'That's enough now,' Fred said, grabbing the child firmly by the arm.

'Ouch,' Enzo whined, and that was all it took for Fred to get angry with himself.

'Stop your nonsense right now and stay with me until we get to camp. You are not allowed to play in the woods with the others. That's your punishment. That's it – march!'

Enzo's dark eyes flared. He looked from Fred to Yasmine, and then to Emma. The two little girls felt a buzzing in their chests. They weren't sure whether they wanted to burst into tears or pee their pants. In solidarity, they just held hands.

When the little group arrived at the campsite, Enzo was still being punished, Louis was still a wolf man, and Nathalie was still so pale she seemed to glow with a ghostly phosphorescence in the shadows as the evening fell. Her son Hugo had noticed and had slowly moved away from his classmates and toward her to soothe her with a symbolic hand on her back and comforting words.

'Go have fun, sweetheart,' Nathalie said. 'I'll be fine.'

But Hugo stayed, gripped by an uncertain feeling he didn't understand that was threatening to spread through his entire body, the feeling of suddenly finding himself alone, without his mother, in a hostile forest that was growing darker, surrounded by people incidental to his life who could never understand or take the place of his mother, who, despite her frequent absences, always listened to him, always heard what he had to say, and was the only one who could anticipate his needs and allay his fears. Hugo didn't say any of this, not even to himself, but because of the irrational fear that an animal was crouched not far off in the bushes, somewhere, anywhere, lying in wait for him, the feeling was gnawing at him. That his mother could die, or at least disappear, leaving him forever lost and alone in the unsettling forest of his peers, was a possibility he had never really considered, let alone felt in his bones, until this faint twilight.

The campsite was made up of a half-dozen large tents solidly anchored to the ground and the surrounding trees, a plywood shed with the food stores for their stay, kitchen utensils, a first-aid kit, and an assortment of tools to deal with the problems that could arise in the great outdoors. A long, rough wooden table, lined with two benches hewn from a tree trunk, and a circular firepit with stones blackened from the many campfires the site had seen made up the spot that was to be home to the twelve children and their three chaperones for three days and three nights. The site remained set up all summer, and dozens of groups of children went there to discover the joys of the outdoors.

After dropping their backpacks, the children flitted around the campsite like a flock of starlings, while Sandra and Fred approached Nathalie, whose legs were now barely holding her up. She was trembling and sweating, feeling the effects of wind and thermal air movements unrelated to the coolness of the late day, of which the humidity of the soil and the moss was taking advantage in the growing dusk to rise up from the ground, filling the space with acrid and strangely metallic odours. The teacher placed his hand on the young woman's feverish brow and said that there was no point in her staying.

'I'm going to call my husband,' Sandra said. 'He can come pick you up and drive you home. You can't spend the night outdoors, the state you're in.'

Nathalie nodded her head at each remark, unable to signal her agreement in any other way.

'I'll stay with the children,' Fred said, 'and you go with Nathalie to the road. Normally, I shouldn't be alone with so many children, but this is an emergency.'

He heard a cry. Then a burst of laughter.

'And you'll be back soon,' Fred added.

'Can I go play with the others now?'

The three adults turned and saw Enzo's puny profile, standing beside them as if he had not left their side since his punishment had started.

'No, Enzo, no,' Fred said, distracted. 'Now's not the time.'

Enzo's face grew even darker, twitching with the rage that swept over it, his teeth clenched so hard they could have shattered.

What's with him? the child thought. *What is going on in that moron's head?*

What was going on in Fred's head was all the worst scenarios imaginable, which kept crashing into one another, the result of the decision he had just made. But was there another option? Calling an ambulance to come to the campsite to avoid finding himself alone, even for a few minutes, in charge of twelve children, which was formally prohibited? They could hardly bother doctors, maybe forcing them to use a vehicle specially designed for the woods, just for a stomach bug. And at school, with his double class, he was often alone with twenty children. No one ever said anything about that, certainly not the Department of Education, which kept eliminating teaching positions and filling up classes like chicken battery cages. It was only for a few minutes. The children would eat and, when Sandra returned, they wouldn't even know she had been gone. Nothing would happen, Fred thought. Nothing ever happened, so this time would be like all the others. Nothing would happen this time either.

'She really isn't feeling well,' Sandra said to her husband on the phone. 'Yes, right away.'

The cry of a bird in the treetops nearby, followed by a furious flapping of wings, triggered a chorus of alarmed squeals, along with mocking laughter from the children.

Sandra waited a few seconds for calm to be restored to explain to her husband how to find the spot where the bus had dropped them off.

'No, don't delay. Come right away. We'll be waiting for you on the shoulder.'

Then she hung up and said to Fred and Nathalie, 'Let's go before it gets dark.'

Olivier put his glass of whisky down on the coffee table and heaved an alcohol-soaked sigh.

'Christ, I don't believe this,' he grumbled, his eyes closed, while in his skull his brain seemed to be spinning as if in reverse on a rickety roller coaster. Three, four? How many drinks had he had time for since the glorious late afternoon when he waved goodbye to his wife and daughter through the window of the bus that was taking them off to the depths of the forest for a few days? Four? Five? It hadn't mattered, since, theoretically, the weekend stretched before him like a giant playground with no one to ask him questions, monitor his blood alcohol, or insist that he express himself intelligibly. No limits, total freedom. He thought he would have a few days to go back to the times of the peaceful solitary binge, accompanied by moronic TV shows and the odd porn video. It had been too long. When was he last able to lock himself away and think only about himself, his privacy, with no one watching, no judgment, no worries to dull his pleasure? Obviously it was before Jade was born, maybe even before he married Sandra, in the few months before they were living together, when his future wife was working nights at the hospital. He remembered now, not a particular day, but that feeling that sent shivers down his spine when he closed the door of the little car, watched his girlfriend recede in the distance, and climbed the three floors alone to his apartment, wondering what he should do with his night of freedom. At the time, the solitary hours stretched out like brief but enjoyable vacations, and he never realized how difficult it would be to recreate this innocent oasis once he was a husband and a father. Yet Olivier was hardly a nonconformist. His colleagues and friends found him too serious, often uptight, too much a stickler about the rules to live life to the fullest. But today he realized that he missed those evenings stretching before him when he didn't have to answer to anyone but himself. Not to indulge in any shameful perversion, but just to be alone and pleasantly idle. Olivier loved his wife. He loved his daughter. But when he found out that they were going camping in the Morvan, he couldn't help but rejoice inside at the idea of reconnecting, even for a few hours, with that pleasant frisson, the feeling of having no responsibilities, no limits, no social obligations.

Once the bus had turned the corner, Olivier had rushed to the car to go to the supermarket one town over – not the one his wife went to, where the cashiers would be sure to snitch on him – to buy a bottle of whisky. He was surprised he couldn't find the bargain brand he liked back in the day; had it been that long, he wondered, that he had remained an upstanding, responsible person, a good husband and father? The time had come to show a little gumption, he thought as he smiled and grabbed a bottle from the last shelf of the section, from the ones that were much more expensive than the rotgut he used to drink and that had an anti-theft device fastened to their necks. He picked up a case of twelve Trappist beers and went to the cash like an outlaw, astonished that no one stopped to handcuff him. Then he drove home, religiously sticking to the speed limit, carefully parking his car in the garage, which he closed and locked behind him, and, after putting the beer in the fridge, he flopped down on the couch with a resonant sigh. For many minutes, there was nothing. The television was off, the radio too, the neighbourhood was calm, no phones were ringing, no dogs barking. Even the boiler that normally hummed in every room of the house seemed dormant because of the warm, summer-like temperatures. Not a voice, not a cry, nothing to disrupt the moment that Olivier was delighting in. Then he opened his eyes again, grabbed the bottle of whisky from the plastic bag at his feet, took a large glass from the china cabinet, and poured the amber liquid into it. Happiness was found in tranquility, he thought, making a face as he downed a first gulp.

When Sandra called to ask him to rush to come pick up Nathalie, at first Olivier didn't understand, then he mentally struggled against what he was hearing, as if in a nightmare he couldn't wake up from, until he realized there was no escape: either he took the car and meekly complied, or he admitted to his wife that he had had too much to drink to get behind the wheel. Either way, disaster loomed, but the first option, dangerous though it might be, at least allowed him to hope for a miracle, and a bit of composure could get him out of this tight spot. He didn't think he felt too bad. His temples weren't throbbing, his head wasn't caught in a vise, his vision was perfect, and while he couldn't remember how many drinks he'd had, he thought that was down to absent-mindedness and not because he was drunk, as his gait didn't seem to be affected as he headed to the medicine cabinet in the bathroom. Just to be sure, he swallowed an aspirin to deal with any possible side effects, then walked to the garage with the assurance of a man who hasn't yet realized he is drunk.

'*O*nce upon a time there was a mouse, a tiny little mouse that lived in a little hole dug in the side of the mountain. At the foot of the mountain, a sparkling blue sea gently caressed a thin strip of pebble beach, shaded here and there by kindly pines and huge grey rocks eroded by the wind and the salt.'

'Fred, where's my mom?' little Jade asked.

'She'll be back soon,' Fred answered. 'I told you, she's gone to take Hugo's mom back because she's sick.'

'Yes, but when is she coming back?' the child pressed.

'Soon, Jade. She shouldn't be long now. I'm sure she'll be here before the end of the story.'

But Fred had started to wonder what Sandra was doing. The road wasn't that far away, was it? Had her husband gotten lost? Had Nathalie run into a problem? *No*, he thought. *Sandra has her phone. She would have called if anything were up. But still, it had been a while. I've had time to feed the children, get them into their pyjamas, and start the story. Maybe I should call. Where did I put my phone?*

'Fred! Tell us the story!' Mathis cried, making the teacher, who was lost in thought, jump.

'Yes, the scary story,' Enzo added. 'So far, it's not scary at all. I know stories that are much scarier than that.'

In a circle around the gently crackling campfire, the children were in pyjamas, curled up under blankets and listening for the creaking of the trees, the distant rustlings of forest animals, and all sorts of noises, shadows, and breezes, most of which were the products of their imagination. None of them had reacted to Enzo's obvious threat, thinking that Fred's story, but also the absence of a story, was already scary enough, not to encourage their sadistic classmate to plunge them into even more terror. Their first night away from their parents, their first night outdoors, in the middle of a nature park teeming with threats, none of them would be able to take any more without dissolving into tears and begging to be taken home.

'Okay, okay,' Fred said, before clearing his throat. 'Every day the little mouse saw the majestic seabirds gliding over the waves, flying to the top of the mountain, and occasionally coming down to the beach to dry their ample wings wet from the sea spray. Full of admiration and envy, the little mouse refused to accept her status as a simple rodent and swore that one day she too would be able to take to the air, cross the ocean to see the world from on high, and finally stop crawling on the ground. So one morning, she took matters in hand – or rather, in paw' – the children laughed nervously – 'and went to the beach to talk to one of the birds. "Mr. Bird," she said, in her little mousey voice. "I'm sorry to bother you, but can you tell me how it is that you fly?" The bird, which was an old seagull with a chipped beak, eyed the mouse in disdain and replied that there was no point in a mouse learning to fly, because to fly, you little twit, you need wings, and you have only four tiny, grotesque feet. "Of course," the mouse said calmly, "but if I had wings, could you teach me to fly?" "You don't learn to fly," the old seagull answered. "You are made to fly, like the birds and the wasps, or to crawl, like the slugs and the rats like you. It's the nature of things, and there's nothing you can do to change it." So the little mouse politely said goodbye to the seagull, without letting her anger show, and went back to her hole, cursing the bird and trying to think of a way to prove him wrong. She got up on her hind legs and spread her front paws wide, imitating and mocking the old seagull drying himself. That was when she figured out how she too could have wings and fly. So every day, rather than nibbling on nuts and fruit with the other mountain mice, the little mouse held a stone in her back paws and spent the day hanging from a pine branch. Every day, she was sure of it, her front legs were growing longer, and after an entire year of suffering, stretched by the weight of the stone, she had to change branches because her feet were touching the ground. And every morning, she spread her legs wide like the old seagull drying itself and noticed that her skin was stretching too, losing its fur, and becoming translucent in spots. *They may not be feathers*, she said to herself, *but soon they will be wings.*

'A bat!' Lucas cried out triumphantly. 'It's turning into a bat!'

'Of course, everyone knows that,' Raphael said. 'We've known for a long time it was going to turn into a bat.'

'Oh, shut up, you did not,' Lucas said. 'I just told you, so that's how you figured it out.'

'That's not true!' Raphael shouted.

'Settle down, everyone!' Fred said. 'Otherwise, the story ends now and you will all be sent to your tents.'

'Nooooo!' the twelve children cried, in the same whining tone.

'Okay,' Fred went on. 'Then I don't want to hear any more comments until the end of the story.'

'Fred?'

'Yes, Mathis?'

'I have to pee.'

'Well, go on then. We'll wait for you before we finish the story.'

'Fred?'

'Yes, Mathis?'

'Can Hugo come with me?'

'Pfft, chicken,' Enzo squealed.

'Enzo!' Fred yelled. 'I told you I didn't want to hear any more from you tonight! Hugo, go with Mathis. We'll wait for you.'

Once they were outside the halo of orange light cast by the campfire, Mathis grabbed his friend's arm. Yes, he may be a scaredy-cat, let Enzo say what he liked, but he was about to pee his pants, and he wouldn't have left the group on his own to face the darkness closing in on them like a cold vise for anything in the world.

'Are you sure he understood where we were?' Nathalie asked weakly.

'He understood,' Sandra replied curtly, standing at the edge of the road, scanning the pavement, which the evening was turning into black velvet carpet.

Nathalie was sitting on the trunk of a huge tree that had fallen at the roadside, and the dampness of both the dead wood and the night air, and the idea that she was dozens of kilometres from a toilet worthy of the name, were the last straw for her rioting digestive system. If the guy didn't arrive in the next five minutes, she would just have to slide to the other side of the trunk, pull down her shorts and her underwear, and spend the night there, laid up, painfully eliminating what remained of her bile and her propriety.

'There he is,' Sandra said, with a mix of relief, pride, and irritation.

The Renault Espace was advancing slowly, its trajectory revealing nothing of the driver's condition. Yet the route had been long and the driving difficult for Olivier, whose confidence during the first few kilometres had given way to a disconcerting drowsiness, as the fatigue and the alcohol started to wreak havoc on his senses and reflexes. At dusk, the shapes seemed to mutate and twist; the road made imaginary obstacles appear and holes close up as soon as you looked at them. Minute by minute, the whisky had methodically attacked his lucidity, as he alternated between anxiety, hands gripping the steering wheel, eyes wide on the blurry shadows, and total loss of vigilance, on the verge of sleep. Opening the vehicle's four windows wide, letting the wind whip his face and the cold stimulate his body, was how he managed to stay alert, but he didn't allow himself to be taken in by it: he had experienced this sort of state before, moments when, after having toyed with you and your feeling of invincibility, alcohol took hold of your body for good. Once you got to that stage, no cool wind, no cold shower, no strong coffee could do anything for you. You were drunk, and only sleep and the promise of a painful awakening would fix you. But Olivier knew that his bed was still a long way off and that there were plenty of trials ahead of him, the most tricky of them having just appeared, in the distance, planted like a stake on the shoulder, arms crossed in the beam of the headlights. He hurried to close the windows, slowed down, then manoeuvred the car to the right to try to park. The Renault Espace rolled a few dozen metres with one wheel in the grass, the other on the road, and stopped its slow advance beside Sandra, who looked decidedly irritated. Fearing he would give himself away, Olivier didn't get out of the car, just rolling down the passenger window to greet his wife.

'It took you long enough,' she grumbled. 'What were you doing?'

Olivier gathered what remained of his wits and, enunciating as best he could, lied, saying he had to make a long detour to fill up. Nathalie got off the tree trunk and stumbled to the car, scrambling behind Sandra, who was opening the door for her. Olivier started in surprise when he saw his passenger, pale, her skin slightly clammy, her slim shoulders and thighs, contrasting so clearly with his wife's chubby, lumpy silhouette. Hadn't he seen her before? At school, maybe, but he went there so rarely and couldn't remember. Or maybe it was somewhere else. At the grocery store where he liked to go with Sandra, not to do groceries or take an interest, but to take advantage of one of the rare outings he allowed himself, aside from alternating weekly visits to his parents and his wife's parents. It wasn't clear, and he doubted that in his condition he could retrieve this hypothetical memory before the next day, so he tried no more and simply said hello to Nathalie, before asking her where he should take her.

'Have a good weekend, dear,' he said to Sandra.

This time his speech was so erratic that the two women knit their brows in unison. They didn't look at one another, but both knew that tone of voice only too well. Was he totally sloshed, they both wondered at exactly the same moment, the moment when the electric window was going up and the car was starting off down the dark road, the bends of which snaked through thousands of tree trunks that were mortal threats to a car going at top speed.

T he bat story was starting to seriously get on Enzo's nerves. They had been promised scary stories, with monsters and ghosts, whispered around the fire in the groans of the night. Instead, they were stuck with a stupid moral fable, the end of which, there could be no further doubt, would laud the tenacity and self-denial of the brave little rodent, who rejected the inevitable, despite it all. *Pathetic*, was how Enzo summed it up in his mind. His father had always told him, and his father knew what he was talking about: you shouldn't get big ideas. Imagining you can change the world when you come from the bottom, imagining you can fly when you are just a garbage-eating rat, is not just pointless; it's painful to have to bang your snout against all the walls of a labyrinth that can't be cracked.

I mean, what is going on in this guy's head? Enzo thought. *If you're a mouse, have fun with your mouse friends, tease them, shove them, bash them about the head until they fall into line, and become the mouse king, a king without a crown, the undisputed king, the one who does whatever he wants, who never lets anyone step on his toes or lay down the law. Living this good life, why would you want to fly? And why suffer so long without being sure of the result? Pathetic, every last one of them,* Enzo sniggered, raking the embers of the campfire with a dead branch.

There: the tip of the branch finally went up in flames. He pulled it out of the fire and considered the flame dancing on the end of the stick. Mathis and Hugo were taking their time coming back from the bathroom, and Lucas was using the opportunity to strut about, saying that he was clearly the smartest in this class, since he had so quickly figured out the tale. Unnoticed, Enzo had moved the flaming stick in Lucas's direction, perhaps not to hurt him, but at least to put an end to his tiresome monologue. The little flame slipped under Lucas's thigh – he was sitting cross-legged – and in a few seconds, the leg of his pyjamas had started to smoke. The faint feeling of heat changed into a slight pinch and, once his brain had made the connection between the thin wisps of smoke and the pain on the back of his thigh, Lucas jumped up, screaming and stamping his feet, his hands frantically slapping his thighs, his torso, and his bum, as if he were afraid he were already a human torch. The event provoked two different reactions among the children: some of them couldn't help but laugh at the ridiculousness of the scene; others were yelling and gesticulating, not knowing why, or perhaps to finally release the pressure and the terrors that the night had bubbling up inside them. Enzo was the only one who was stoic, smiling through the chaos, looking satisfied with his piece of choreography, a look that wasn't lost on Fred, as the teacher leapt on his pupil, blanket in hand, to put out the pyjama fire. Alerted by the noise of the shouting, Mathis and Hugo rushed back from the toilet to find the camp's calm restored, their classmates gathered around Fred, who was examining Lucas's minor burn.

'Jade's mother still isn't back?' Hugo asked.

But no one heard him. Much more than for the end of the story or Enzo's umpteenth rude remark, Hugo was impatiently waiting for Sandra to come back to tell him his mother was fine or, at least, that she was on her way to the doctor's, who would soon make her better. But Sandra hadn't come back to camp, whether of her own volition or not.

It wasn't that complicated, she thought, stumbling on the uneven path; she just had to go straight, then turn right near the big pile of rocks. But it was dark now, and without a flashlight, the only source of light being the screen of her phone that she had to keep turning back on, maybe she had got the wrong pile of rocks and hadn't turned at the right place. But it wasn't that serious. She would just have to double back until she reached the right junction. She knew that the forest roads were laid out in a grid, so finding the way was never that hard and, in the worst-case scenario, she could always call Fred. But what would she say? She was less and less sure of where she was. Was she getting closer to camp, or farther away? In the faint halo from the cellphone she was holding up in front of her, she wondered whether this trail was really taking her deeper into the forest. Or had she inadvertently left the waymarked routes and ended up blindly following a trail like the one the deer, foxes, and boars had cut through the tangle of the underbrush? If her feckless husband hadn't done what he did, she wouldn't be here, she thought. If she hadn't spent the first hundred or so metres of her return trip mentally tearing a strip off him for having gotten hammered as soon as her back was turned, she would definitely have been more focused and would have had no trouble finding the goddamn pile of rocks. *What an idiot*, she thought, *I mean, what an idiot!* That was pretty much what Enzo was thinking too, when Fred had escorted him to his tent, ordering him to bed for the night in front of his classmates, since he was now being punished, deprived of the end of the evening.

'Whatever. Your story was dumb,' Enzo spat as a final taunt.

Would he end up getting the smack even he thought he had had coming for so long? Still nothing. Without answering, Fred had pulled the tent's zipper closed and walked back to the campfire and the children, who were starting to get sleepy.

Sleepy was not exactly the word for what Olivier was feeling. Stupor or torpor, perhaps, that moment when physical suffering stops you from distinguishing whether images, sounds, and voices are coming from the real world or are the fruit of our mind.

'Have you lived around here long?' 'What do you do for a living?' 'How are things?' 'Is it a growing industry?' 'Are you married?' 'In a relationship?' 'Divorced?' The screech of tires. The white form of a quadruped in the distance at the edge of the headlights. Did he ask all these questions? Did he get answers? Was Nathalie even awake? Her head was resting against the window, which was lowered a little.

'What happened?' 'Did you eat something that was off?' 'A stomach flu is no fun.' 'When you get home, you should make yourself a nice bowl of rice. It settles the stomach.'

Between questions, to which he didn't really expect an answer, but which kept him awake, Olivier focused on the blinding white of the road signs. Their contours were fuzzier, their shapes less straight, the letters jumping around, making for unlikely town names: Bourmeult, Galny, Apalonne-le-Clocher. He didn't think he had left the main road on his way here, so he figured he wouldn't need to turn off. But Gouloux, Glux, Onlay. *How could they have given towns such names? I must be losing it*, he thought. *I have to pull myself together. I have a passenger, and she's sick. I have to get her home safe and sound. That face. I know her. I'm sure I know her.*

'Are you feeling any better?' 'Do you want me to roll down the window a little more?' 'We've met before, haven't we?' 'Do you ever take your son to the rec centre?' 'I go there to pick up Jade. I don't drop her at school often, because I start work early, but I do go to the rec centre. Maybe we've seen each other there.'

Olivier gave a sudden start, which made him grip the steering wheel. A muffled noise and a strange vibration had pulled him from his drowsiness. Or had he nodded off for a second? The car's trajectory had gradually taken it toward the shoulder, and he had to swerve left to stop the Renault Espace from ending up in the ditch, narrowly missing it. Glancing in Nathalie's direction, Olivier saw, reassured, that she didn't seem to have noticed anything. She must be fast asleep.

'Are you asleep?' 'You must need rest.' 'It can't be easy bringing up a young boy on your own.'

The grey carpet of the road changed colour whenever Olivier pressed or lifted his foot from the accelerator. *It's like a mechanical paintbrush*, he thought.

'I have Sandra, so we can help each other when things get rough. It must be hard on your own. I'm trying to imagine what it's like. Without anyone to lean on. No one to answer the questions you can't. And we're getting older. Hate to say it, but I've been thinking about it a little today. I'm a bit like you, you know. I'm not exactly alone, but what difference does that make? I'm getting older. We're all getting older, and every day that passes takes us a little further from the freedom we once had and could have again. All the people around us, all the pictures, friends, colleagues, and strangers showing off how happy they are and what they've achieved; that may be the hardest thing, don't you think?'

The forest was growing inside Olivier's head. Branches were climbing up his torso, roots were breaking through the floor of the car interior and winding around his calves. Whether or not he pressed the accelerator changed nothing further in his surroundings, the sounds, or the colours. He unconsciously concluded that he must be stopped, so there was no more danger. Parking and spending the night there might be a good idea. Particularly since Nathalie didn't seem to be in any discomfort anymore. She was asleep, wasn't she? 'Time passing us by. Solitude. With everyone else thriving and seemingly enjoying fulfilling existences. That's the hard part, don't you think? You must feel it sometimes, feel alone and irritated at night, when the kid is in bed, and you can hear the laughter of people having a good time from the bar down the street? You must think about your body and your beauty too, and tell yourself that you won't be this beautiful for much longer, that everything is sagging and going slack, your breasts of course, a bit – but who sees them out of their bra anyway – but your ass mainly, its shape changing relentlessly, and no jogging or workout at the gym snatched from the mayhem of the week can change that. And maybe you tell yourself that, in the end, your child was a mistake, and the life you didn't quite choose took you down the wrong path. Don't you ever want to start over? To go back to being the child our children are today and make choices other than the ones we made? Good or bad, just other choices. Has someone told you you don't get a second chance? That once you've headed down a road, resolutely, sadly, you can't go back?'

An owl gliding through the trees. The fluorescent flash of a trail sign nailed to a tree trunk. Sandra didn't panic. Sandra was a rational person. If she couldn't find the camp, so be it. She would just have to lean back against a tree, try to sleep a little while waiting for daybreak, and find the children once she could see something. Find that stupid pile of rocks. It was so simple. Then turn right. These dirt roads were perfectly straight, how could she have gotten lost? Hundreds of walkers came here to unwind, to meander in the spring, pick mushrooms at the end of the summer. Had she even once seen in the papers a report of an incident here? A lost hiker? A forest ranger attacked by a wild animal? No. Nothing of the sort. This was hardly the German Black Forest or the Congolese jungle. At worst, you could end up walking in circles for a few hours, but getting lost never to be found again? It couldn't happen, although in the dark of the woods and the chill of the night, in the worrisome concert of scratching and cracking, the curious sounds of twigs snapping a few metres behind her – could a twig snap so crisply without a human foot coming down on it? – Sandra had her doubts. What if she were being followed? What if someone had intentionally obscured the pile of rocks so she would get lost? There were forest rangers here. Who knew the trails and clearings better than them? Isolation could have driven one of them mad, starved for sensation, reverting to his animal nature for a night, if not physically then at least in his mind, hunter and game, predator and prey, and then he would have seen, miraculously, a target in the sights of his madness, and the hunt would have begun. He just had to follow her, at a distance, and then closer and closer – where could she escape to anyway, if she were to detect his presence? – less and less discreetly, until perhaps she would panic and finally run out of energy, collapsing exhausted on the spongy ground to await her fate like a wounded doe. She had never seen anything of the sort in the paper, but Sandra was a rational person, and she knew that just because something hadn't happened before didn't mean it would never happen. There was a first time for everything. Had no one ever gotten lost in this forest? This could be the night. Had no one ever been slaughtered by a forest ranger gone mad? This could be the night.

'There is a first time for everything, children. This is what the little mouse said now that her legs had grown enough to touch the walls of the small cave when she stretched them. Perhaps no mouse had ever flown, but that didn't mean that no mouse would ever fly. She looked up at the blue sky shining outdoors and the tranquil streams of garlands of fluff, and she remembered the awful words of the old seagull: You don't learn to fly, you are either made to fly or you aren't. This was the day. She had done all she could. Her legs were already as long as they would get, and the thin, furless membrane that dangled below looked like the sail of a boat. It was now or never. Either she could fly or she couldn't. So the little mouse came out of the cave and climbed onto an oblong rock that jutted out into the void.

She took in the magnificent landscape, the cool blue she had always dreamed of finding herself in, an endless playground and the backdrop to adventure that seabirds flew hither and thither across. What if she could join them? What if this were the day?'

All the children around the campfire held their breath as Fred paused artfully in his story. All the children except one, who couldn't have cared less about finding out whether or not the mouse could fly, or even whether she burst when stepped on or whether she smelled like merguez when flambéed. Enzo hadn't even tried to sleep. He was just lying on his back, eyes wide open, like he sometimes did when frustration had too powerful a grip on him – not to calm or collect himself, but on the contrary to enjoy feeling his rage boil inside him, to shove it down, and to stoke it and make it ten times stronger. He ruminated, he trembled, he gnashed his teeth: second by second, he was stockpiling an increasingly terrifying amount of dark, hateful energy. He became a little weapon that could scare even adults, a crowbar, a spiked mace, a bomb, a potential threat that the slightest thing could trigger, and that thing was him. He was the only one who knew how to use the weapon that he was, and he got complete satisfaction from it, a certainty in his power that little boys of six feel, that plenty of adults desire but never achieve. To be master of his destiny, sure of his freedom – who could truly claim such things? Don't you agree, Nathalie? You find a job, you get married, you have kids and responsibilities: where is the freedom in that? Before you become an adult, everything is off limits, and, once you become one, you aren't allowed to do anything because you have to be responsible. When in life are we finally free? For good?

In the beam of the headlights, the trees blurred into one, into nothing more than green and brown magma, which the car seemed to float through in slow motion. *Freedom*, Olivier thought. *When are we free? Maybe we never truly are*, he said, or maybe just thought, without having the presence of mind to express it out loud. Maybe true moments of freedom are fleeting, and you have to know how to seize them when they present themselves, with no thought for what is the right thing to do, the responsible thing to say.

'Yes, Olivier,' Nathalie said. 'I couldn't agree more: true freedom is all around you, all the time. You just have to look for it and seize the moment when it presents itself.'

Olivier was stunned, not necessarily to see Nathalie punctuate her comment with a flirtatious wink, but that her answer repeated to the word the sentence he had just imagined. Or had he actually said it? It didn't really matter. What was important now was the texture of the skin of the young woman seated next to him, her delicate shoulders, her slim thighs, the drops of perspiration in the hollow of her cleavage. What was important was a fleeting moment of total freedom that seemed within reach and that he could not fail to seize. Did he dare? Was it appropriate? Surely not. This was nothing like the times when he drank alone at home. This was adultery. That was the word for it and, morally, there was nothing right about it.

Finally! He remembered where he had seen her before! It wasn't at school or at the rec centre or at the supermarket.

He had seen her delicate shoulders and her slim thighs on his computer screen, one night when Jade was asleep and Sandra wasn't home, one of those evenings when his only company, his only distraction, was an endless succession of TV series downloaded illegally and porn he watched without partaking in, for fear of being caught with his pants around his ankles, dick in hand before the spectacle of a young Russian, Polish, or Californian woman being serviced by one or more partners. Of course, that was where he knew her from. Of course, it was all coming back to him now, as he studied his passenger's features, her head resting against the window, eyes closed. Wait, hadn't she just spoken? Winked at him? Why pretend to be asleep now? Maybe it was a game, one of those games porn actresses know how to play so well. After all, he thought, cheating on his wife with a woman like this wasn't really cheating. It was her job, after all. There was no commitment. It was like a game. Like when Sandra's sister the hairdresser cut his hair at home, and, of course, didn't charge him anything. Pay? Oh, no, that would be unseemly. No, just pleasure shared between two discreet adults. At the perfect moment, now, yes, here it was. This was the moment. This was it. This was the moment of freedom he had to seize. Maybe the best moment of all. A weekend without his wife or daughter, a call in the night, and here he was driving through the middle of nowhere with a porn actress at his side. It was today. This was the moment, Olivier thought, suddenly as brave as a little mouse that throws herself into the void without knowing whether she was made to fly. *Have I had the courage to seize an opportunity just once in my life? To do something extraordinary? To live in the moment, damn the torpedoes?*

It's now or never, he thought, to further convince himself, slipping his hand between Nathalie's thighs.

'She can fly! She can fly!' Fred repeated, to the children's applause. 'For the first time in the history of the world, a mouse was flying! People had seen squirrels glide and small rodents be carried on the wind, but this was something different entirely. The little mouse hadn't had to learn. She simply felt the air under her front legs, and her natural strength carried her. She managed to steer, ascend, and dive, so spirited and agile that she seemed to rival the big birds that had been flying since they were young. Speaking of which, wasn't that the featherless silhouette of the old seagull in the distance, coasting on an updraft? "Seagull! Seagull! Look at me, Seagull!" she cried. "I did it! I'm flying, just like you and your friends!" "You are!" the seagull answered, looking surly. "You are one stubborn mouse." "Stubborn and flying," the little mouse added. "True," said the seagull. "And now that you are flying, you can follow me to learn the laws of the skies." "The laws of the skies?" asked the mouse. "Follow me," was all the seagull said, diving toward a precipitous ledge on which were crammed dozens of seagulls, albatrosses, pigeons, crows, even a few sparrows. The old seagull and the little mouse touched down in the middle of the winged assembly, and silence fell when the birds noticed the curious interloper. "My friends," the seagull began, "I have brought you this strange creature to teach her the laws of the skies." The little mouse puffed out her chest, proud to be part of such a marvellous family.'

In his tent, Enzo was grumbling about being shunned.

"'Birds have always flown," the seagull continued, "and

they have always been the masters of the air. We let insects fly so we can eat them without having to land.'"

In the little mouse's stomach and the stomachs of the children around the campfire, there was an unpleasant stirring. Something was wrong; they all felt it.

"'We have often encountered stubborn creatures who wanted to fly at our side, and what did we do?'"

"'We taught them the laws of the skies!' the birds cried.

"'Precisely,' the old seagull said, setting his heavy webbed foot on the mouse's tiny paw. "We taught them the laws of the skies. Do you want us to teach you the laws of the skies, flying mouse?'"

'Trying surreptitiously to free his paw, the mouse spluttered and, gripped by a sinister feeling, didn't quite know what to answer.

"'I … I don't know," she managed to say.

"'What do you mean, you don't know?" the old seagull said, scolding. "You went to all the trouble of joining us in the air. It took you so long to become the first and only flying mammal. Now you can fly, we won't deny it, but you have to learn the laws.'"

"'Law number one,' said the assembly of birds.

"'The skies belong to birds and birds alone,' the seagull said, snapping his dented beak a few centimetres from the mouse's snout.

"'Law number two,' the birds continued.

"'Anything that is not a bird and that flies through the skies is considered bird food.'

'The mouse tried to break free by pulling on her paw with all her might, but the old seagull kept its grip firm.

"'Law number three,' said the gulls, the albatrosses, the sparrows, the crows, and all the other scary winged creatures, their circle gradually closing around their prey.

"'What cannot be eaten by the birds and still flies should not be allowed to admire the wonders of the sky,' said the seagull, staring at the mouse in hostility.

'There was silence on the ledge.

"'What does … what does that mean?' the mouse stammered.

"'It means,' the old seagull replied, "that we will allow you to fly, but you will never again see the sun's rays."

'Suddenly, the old bird jammed the tip of his beak in the little mouse's eye.' Around the campfire, the children who were dozing off jumped, and some screamed in horror and disgust. To calm the rising clamour, Fred continued, raising his voice, and while the children wanted to scream a cathartic scream into the night, they also wanted to hear how the story ended.

"'From this point forward,' the old seagull said, "your eyes shall see no more."

'One after the other, the birds on the ledge took turns pecking at the flying mouse: in the eyes, on the nose, all over the little rodent's face, which was bleeding, splitting, growing deformed. From the scarlet, oozing, gaping hole that had once been her mouth, but that no longer looked like one, the martyred mouse emitted a piercing, unbroken wail.

"'You will no longer see the day,' the old seagull continued, "you will crawl along the ceiling of caves, waiting for the night, and you will feed on night insects and the pollen of flowers that open only in the dark."

'The little mouse shrieked, and then shrieked louder still,

from the pain of the pecking that wouldn't stop, but also from sadness, an endless, bottomless despair at no longer being able to admire the sea from the skies that she had spent so long conquering.

"'Those are the laws of the skies," the seagull said, "and now that you know them, leave this place and go to the damp, dirty caves where vermin who learned them before you live."

'The little mouse felt the large bird remove his foot from hers. But she was aware of nothing else, because she couldn't see anything, and that horrible, piercing, awful scream kept ringing in her ears, her own scream, which came from the depths of her wounded throat, such a penetrating cry, which held so much sadness that no one could hear, or at least no one but her, because she alone could understand how filled it was with woe.'

It was a strange, unpleasant sensation to scream for yourself alone, to scream silently. Nathalie didn't do it for long. When she woke with a start, horrified that a hand was gripping her crotch, her shrill voice filled the car, but in less than four seconds, the car went off the road and plunged into a pond a few metres down, the shattered windshield letting in thousands of litres of stagnant green water, and instantly her cry was stilled in the mouthful of the cold water, not even understanding that she was dying or why. Screaming for oneself, screaming silently, is a curious sensation, and there are few things more unpleasant than the endless frustration of not being able to release one's rage, one's fear, hatred, or pain by letting loose a liberating wave that would echo for kilometres. The car came to rest at the bottom of the pond,

Nathalie dead in the death seat and Olivier at the wheel, his skull fractured on the metal door that the impact had hurled him into. The duckweed gradually settled back into place on the pond's surface, the eddies and the ripples slowly disappeared, and calm was restored to this corner of the forest while, a few kilometres away, Hugo and Jade's class, Océane, Louis, and Mathis's class, Lucas's class, and Enzo's class were getting restless, chattering and shouting their bafflement and fear, picturing the end of the tragic story of a little mouse whose efforts – how could such a thing be? – would forever be in vain.

Fred sat down to swallow a mouthful of cold water and clear his throat. He listened for a few minutes to the children's comments, thinking it was a good idea to first let them voice all of their questions and remarks, before bringing the weight of his judgment as an adult and teacher to bear on them. Then he quickly moved a few metres away and tried to find Sandra, whose absence had been niggling at him through the whole story. He was starting to get truly worried. And through his class's excited clamour, he didn't hear the little steps sneak up behind him, nor had he heard the tent zipper that had been pulled down a moment earlier.

'What?' he said, seeing the children looking at him, their little eyes wide and filled with disbelief – or fear? Was it fear too? – and conversations about the destiny of the blind flying mouse were abruptly forgotten. 'What?' is what came to mind because nothing seemed to explain the sudden silence, and then the silence didn't matter quite as much; the reason for the silence and any other mystery here on earth instantly faded to the background of his worrying, because the most important question had just imposed itself with the intransigence of rock and the violence of war. Fred dropped to all fours in shock, stunned and no longer understanding who he was or what he was doing there, in the middle of the woods, with this excruciating pain at the back of his head. With precise, methodical movements, Enzo had slipped around Fred, picked up a large rock, and brought it down on his teacher's head, had struggled to raise it against the black sky of the forest and brought it down a second time on the back of the head of the teacher, who had collapsed on his belly on the ground, as his petrified students looked on. Enzo raised the rock a third time and again brought it down on Fred's head, the cranial bone making a sharp crack. This time, the rock didn't rebound but rested at the point of impact, as if planted in Fred's scalp, and his head gave a final jerk. A blank-faced Enzo then kneeled near the adult's body and again grabbed the rock in his hands to raise it above his head and let it fall in the exact same spot, this time producing a pink-and-grey spatter that stained his pyjamas and his face, which was already flushed with effort. The rock was heavy, and Enzo was still just a child, so he didn't feel strong enough to repeat the gesture as many times as he would have liked. He was already out of breath, and his biceps and shoulders ached, although he didn't want his dumbstruck audience to know it. Mustering all of his energy, he managed to raise the rock once more and let it drop on Fred's exposed brain, raised it again, let it drop with a new sibilant splat – *the same sound as a soaked sponge hitting the ground when Dad washes the car*, he thought – raised it one last time, dropped it one last time on the bloody pulp, brain matter, and bone fragments that were now Fred's head, and finally rolled the weapon of his crime to one side, panting. Yasmine started to cry, silently at first, fat tears rolling down her little pink cheeks, then louder and louder, sniffing and sobbing, trembling and hiccupping more and more uncontrollably, while Enzo stayed bent over his work, plunging his fingers into Fred's massacred brain.

'What is going on in your head,' he repeated, 'eh, Fred? What is going on in your head?' picking up a limp grey piece of brain with the tips of his fingers, studying it with interest, as if it were an unusual plant or an amusing insect, and then tossing it on the ground to take a look at another.

This was the first time any of the children had seen such a thing, and no one knew how to respond, so everyone just went with their first instinct, after a few inevitable minutes of horrified astonishment. Yasmine's muffled sobs changing to resonant, uncontrolled crying was the trigger that roused in each child the need to act. And the first of these actions was to scream again, in unison, as loudly as they possibly could. Screaming and crying, screaming and running, screaming with more power than they had ever had before or would ever have again. Fred's class was no longer Fred's class, because there was no more Fred; this disgusting mess could not be Fred, and now they were no more than children lost at night in heart of the forest.

II

Sandra did her best not to panic. She retraced her steps, branched off down different paths, then down others still, but nothing looked familiar anymore. Basically nothing had ever looked familiar, because the forest during the day is different from the forest in the evening, and different still from the forest at night. As responsible as she was, as much as she was supposed to be a reasonable adult, she felt rise in her something that bore a strong resemblance to a child's sob. Lost, at night, in the middle of the forest, who wouldn't, like her, be enveloped by a spooky mist of lore, the cold stab of fear, thought to be forgotten but still lurking deep down inside, a primal fear of the dark when the bedroom door isn't open a crack, of the wolf that is said to attack children when they are alone, of the thief who sneaks into houses through windows left open in the summer, throwing children in a large burlap sack and carrying them far away from their parents, to sell them or simply devour them. There is also the fear of evil spirits who torment the credulous for kicks, who make beams creak and gutters squeak, the fear of falling asleep and never waking again, the fear of being buried alive, the fear of sinking into quicksand, the fear of being snatched by a shark, the fear of being pursued by a giant beast that makes the ground shake with every footfall. Really, where is there to hide? How do you escape? All the fears that used to fill our days and our imaginations, how can you avoid being suddenly seized by them once again, here, in the dark, with the whispers of the trees and the invisible beasts?

You have to call now, Sandra thought. *Enough pretending you're resourceful. You're lost and you have to tell Fred that you won't reach camp until daybreak, when you can read the numbers marking the trails and can find the ones you must have missed, or crossed, or taken in the wrong direction.* Scrolling through her contacts for the teacher's number, Sandra noticed that she had precious little battery left. Using her phone as a flashlight for the past two hours had probably been a bad idea. She had touched the little green key, and the ringtone started to sound.

Several hundred metres away, in the pocket of the jeans of a headless body, a cellphone started to ring. The sweet melody roused Enzo from his contemplative pose. He lifted his head, looked around, and realized that most of his little classmates had fled. On the other side of the dying campfire was Emma, kneeling next to her friend Yasmine, who was inconsolable. The little girl's face was contorted by her crying, slick with tears and snot, her brimming eyes trained on the orgy of blood and bone that Enzo was wading through.

'It's your fault I was punished,' Enzo said, looking at the girls with a menacing stare.

'Hurry! Hurry!' Emma whispered, tugging on her friend's arm.

Yasmine's sobs ended in a noisy gulp as she looked at the macabre scene before her, terrified: a little boy in sky blue pyjamas, kneeling on the ground, his bum resting on his heels, his hands dripping with blood, his forearms and his sleeves stained with blood, his pyjama top splattered with blood, his knees soaking in an adult's blood, a headless body in the dim, reddish glow of the embers, a pool of black blood spread in the dirt and the pine needles, and murderous, vengeful, reproachful eyes driving into her like the hook of a line he just had to wind in to make her his next victim.

Enzo's expression changed when he heard Fred's cellphone ring again. He bent over the body and patted the pocket where the sound seemed to be coming from.

'Come on! Come on!' Emma begged, and this time Yasmine heard her.

Holding hands, the two little girls leapt to their feet and ran for the nearest trees. Without looking back or checking with each other, they plunged into the darkness of the woods, because there was no darkness scarier than the one about to give chase.

Lucas ran straight ahead as fast as he could, with no regard for anyone, for any of his classmates who were also running, first in the same direction as him, then veering off one by one, Océane, Louis, and Nathan, the three irksome jerks he had never liked, with their weirdo games they never wanted to let anyone in on – let the three of them get lost. He wouldn't be the one to point them in the direction the road lay, that way, to the west, where he knew help could be called, by a passing car, Jade's mother perhaps, adults in any case, who would take things in hand, keep them safe from harm, and put Enzo in jail. No, not jail. He knew they didn't put kids in jail, but somewhere else, something like jail, but for kids, a place where he would be locked up, at any rate, so that he wouldn't be able to hurt anyone anymore, and so that he would be far away from Lucas, as far as possible, forever; that's how much what he had seen had terrified him. Enzo had long scared him, really scared him, since the day he had first seen him, in fact, since the first day at the big school, the day when Lucas with his nice manners had bid a cheerful hello to the classmate walking his way and that classmate had ignored the greeting and continued to walk straight on, violently shoving him, him and his ridiculous politeness. And every day since then, Enzo had made a point of shoving Lucas by way of greeting, sometimes so hard that Lucas landed on his bum on the asphalt of the schoolyard. It was like a ritual, a custom, like some people kiss on both cheeks and others invent complicated greetings with their hands and fingers. Every morning Enzo would shove Lucas, and Lucas alone. It was his special treatment, and every morning, before being shoved, Lucas dreaded the humiliation, fearing he would be hurt when he fell, as he sometimes was, but fearing mostly that the inevitable shove would happen in front of all the other kids at school, that some would laugh and make fun of him. But what terrified him most was that once again he wouldn't have the nerve to say anything, wouldn't respond, wouldn't even defend himself, confirming to everyone that he was indeed an impotent worm you could treat any old way, a daily affirmation that that was his station, his caste, his social status in the schoolyard, until he decided to react. Although some children never do (something he had no way of knowing), and every morning of their lives until their last, they are greeted by terror that knocks them flat, whether blatantly, directly, or not. Long after they have left school, every morning until their last, they wind up flat on their asses, with everyone watching, as they lie frozen in fear, paralyzed by the attack, and then in fear of the next attack, which they know is inevitable. Who had come to his aid since the beginning of the year? Who had had the courage to stand up to Enzo – after all, two people are stronger than one, right? Or three? Or eight? Who had had the guts to stand beside him, even just to help him up? What would it have cost them to hold out a hand and lend some support? Nothing. It would have cost nothing. But no one did, not one of this stupid bunch of green-eyed monsters had ever reached out their hand: Hugo because, after all, it was easy to make fun of the four-eyes who had been reading since his last year of nursery school, Louis and Mathis because they were afraid of ending up in his place and suffering the same fate if they got involved, Nathan because he was too spaced out and may not have realized that Enzo was hurting him, and the big kids from the other classes because they didn't even notice the smaller kids, too caught up in their own business, their own concerns, and their invisible injuries.

No one ever helped me, Lucas thought, running through the woods until he was out of breath, hitting the low branches of evergreen trees, which scratched his face, tripping in the brambles, which shredded his ankles. *No one ever protected me from him, so now I'm not going to protect them either.* And he ran, farther and farther, going deeper and deeper into the jet-black forest, in what he thought was the right direction. He was sure it was, because, he thought, *I may run slower than the others, but I'm the only one running in the right direction, because although I don't know how to fight, I am a lot smarter than the others, and anyway, I was the first to figure out that the mouse was going to turn into a bat, and I will be the first one to find the road, and to flag down a passing car, and call for help, the police or the fire department. I'm the one who will save everyone, thanks to my intelligence, because I'm the only one who remembered that we came from the west and that you have to head west to find the road without taking the trail.* And then Lucas's foot suddenly slipped on the more crumbly ground, and his other foot slid along with it, as if the slope were suddenly much steeper. His pelvis got swept up in the momentum of his legs, which were now parallel to the ground, and his head was thrown backwards and downwards, while his arms flapped wildly in the air, as if trying to regain the balance that was lost. Lucas's bum landed on the rocky ground, and his head banged against something hard, which must have been a rock or the root of a big tree, and the initial impact knocked out the child, whose body was carried along by the momentum of his run and his fall, continuing to tumble and gaining speed over what turned out to be a precipice, which was undoubtedly shallow but deep enough to put the body of an inert child in a deadly position by the time it reached the bottom. Chance and the cruel laws of physics made it such that Lucas landed on his head, and the weight of his body landing broke his cervical vertebrae, severing his spine in a number of places, breaking the cranial bone in the impact and fracturing his left forearm, leaving it in two perpendicular sections, a spectacular injury, the seriousness of which, given the rest of it, was relative. With a spongy snap, Lucas crumpled to the ground after a fall of barely three metres, and his dislocated, immobile body formed a pile of flesh, limbs, and children's clothes, lying together in a surreal order. The impact didn't kill Lucas instantly. His heart kept beating for about ten seconds, the nerves sending a series of brief impulses to disobedient limbs. The brain was the first to cease all activity, as if signalling to the other vital functions that it was over. His body temperature started to drop, slowly, silently, the heat gradually escaping and rising to the treetops, and maybe beyond, to a sky dotted with tranquil stars.

Océane fled with her two constant companions. Stuck to each other like magnets all year, in this moment of horror, crisis, and panic, they had obeyed a simple symbiotic instinct that could be pretty much summed up by this equation: Océane makes a decision, Nathan seconds it, Louis disagrees with Nathan, Océane supports Louis's disagreement and shifts the responsibility to Nathan, Océane makes the decision that Louis just implicitly suggested, Nathan bends to the will of the other two, and the decision is passed. Because they had spent two years together in the same class, playing the same games, taking the same vacation, and spending afternoons at the rec centre, this tacit decision-making process could be executed in barely a few seconds. For the most critical situations – and this one was by far the most critical they had ever faced – it was executed wordlessly, a simple exchange of furtive looks and gestures that were sufficient to express proposals, counter-proposals, and decisions. When Enzo had bashed Fred on the head the second time with his murderous rock and it had become clear the teacher would not be getting back up, it took only a few seconds for the three friends to decide not to follow the group of panicked children but to set off in a different direction. Without an adult, reality suddenly dissolved. Nothing concrete was preventing Océane from truly being a troll hunter and Louis a wolf-man. Nothing, except perhaps the other children, and staying at their side – at least, this was the sense they had of it – didn't mean they couldn't take refuge in a downy hollow of the imagination, a refuge they had a pressing need for at this moment.

So all three had made a break for the woods, not toward a specific point they imagined reaching, but to where no one other than them seemed to want to go, where the trolls with their bark-like skin turned into oak trees to sleep, where fur-covered fairies had the power to burst into a cloud of a thousand tiny feathers to escape their enemies, and where a word that existed in no language opened a door in the middle of nowhere that led straight to the warmth of the duvet, tucked in bed, for the person who knew how to pronounce it.

Hugo had seen the three of them head toward a mysterious part of the forest, but at no point did he try to dissuade them. He hadn't thought either; he just ran to escape the clear, imminent threat, ran in the direction that his mother, Nathalie, had gone, along the trail, unconsciously hoping to find her. Behind him, four children had started running. When you have no idea what to think or do, it is a common reaction to follow in the steps of the person with the most confidence, the one who shows the greatest assurance, who makes a decision, even if just for himself, while others get bogged down in waiting and seeing. So Jade, Raphael, Lilou, and Mathis had taken off running after Hugo, because if Hugo was escaping in that direction, it must be the right one. And Hugo, as often happened under clearly less critical circumstances, had understood that the group had appointed him leader, and he had naturally slowed down to wait for the slowpokes, called out a few encouragements so that no one would give up and force the group to stop or abandon them there. Eventually, realizing after a few hundred metres of running flat out that no one could keep up with him, he decided to go off the trail and find a hiding place where everyone could catch their breath.

As he tramped on the damp leaves and soft moss, Hugo's mind raced, not like an adult's mind would race, even when gripped with panic, but like a child of six's would, with needs, images, and nerves more than with rational conclusions. Hugo wanted to find his mother. His mother was somewhere in the forest, with Jade's mother, because she had not come back. He just had to reach the road, retrace their steps from earlier, and they would be saved. And if his mother had already left, there was always Sandra. But what if they didn't find Sandra? Hugo furrowed his brow, remembered his mother's instructions when she had to go out for a long time in the evening. 'Try to call me. You remember my number?' 'Yes, Mom,' Hugo answered, reciting the ten digits in a single breath. 'And if you can't reach me, if you're hurt, if there's a fire, if you're in danger, if someone is trying to get in the house, you dial 112 – that's a 1, another 1, and a 2 – you wait for them to answer and you tell them what's going on, okay?' Nothing had ever happened the evenings Nathalie wasn't there; Hugo simply waited in fear that one of those terrifying things should happen, his personality no doubt being shaped by the thought that at any moment tragedy could strike, that a threat weighed constantly on every living being, promising to snatch him away someday, to abuse him or snuff him out. And tonight, the tragedy had actually occurred, an evening when, like so many other evenings, Nathalie had left her son alone in the dark. It wasn't really her fault this time, but she had still left him alone in the dark in the middle of the forest, like so many little characters in the stories she never read him. So Hugo automatically thought, *If I don't find her, I have to call her, and if she doesn't answer, I have to call 112, and to do either of these things, I need a phone, and Fred is the only one who has one, so make it to the road, yes, and maybe Mom will still be there, or Jade's mom if we run into her on the trail. But if none of that goes as planned, I have to go back to camp and get Fred's phone, borrow it from him just for a minute, just long enough to reach Mommy, Mommy's voice at the other end of the line, and ask her, beg her, to come get me, even if she is sick, even if she can't stand up yet again, yet another evening, that this once, just this time, she come get me and take me home.* Hugo's foot hit a hard piece of wood. Widening his eyes in the near pitch black of the underbrush, he could make out an imposing mass lying on its side. Even in the daylight, he would have been unable to determine the variety of tree, but what was important now was that the trunk was wide and deep and long enough to serve as a hiding place for him and his four friends.

'Psst!' he signalled to one of his companions who was waiting for him, panting on the path. 'Over here! Don't just stand there!'

Jade was crying. She was calling quietly for her mother. Lilou's lips were parted, her eyes stuck wide open in horror, as if she were still seeing Fred's skull burst open right in front of her, paralyzed in an astonishment that seemed not to want to leave her. Raphael approached Hugo without looking at him, his face dark, the corners of his mouth drooping like a sad clown, on the verge of sobbing or screaming, his lungs burning, his eyes stinging, thinking of gnawing at his fingers, kicking everything around him, maybe drawing his face and silhouette on a piece of paper and ripping it up in rage and hatred to see whether that would bring him any relief. Mathis had finally caught up with them near the tree trunk, trotting, seemingly carefree, looking trusting, as he often did, following his friends as if this were an orienteering class or one of the games the activities coordinators at the rec centre made them play. If the child's head had been cut off, he would probably have continued to jog in the same way, like a decapitated duck, and his face would undoubtedly have that same gullible look as it lay on the ground in a clump of grass.

'Hide in there,' Hugo said, 'and don't make a sound.'

On hearing his words, Jade instantly started to cry, and the four children entered the hollow trunk one after another, on all fours or on their bellies, to be joined straight away by Hugo, who slid in backwards to keep an eye on the goings-on outside.

Inside the tree, the smell of wet wood was overpowering. It was the smell of the forest, and while you notice and savour it while on a Sunday walk, it penetrates and possesses you when you slide into the putrid bowels of one of these plant cadavers. When you are six, and you crawl into the damp insides that crumble under your fingers and wet your palms and knees, and you are in the dark, afraid of never seeing your parents again, or your brothers or sisters, or maybe even the light of day, it smells and feels like the tree is eating you. Come to think of it, what do trees eat? There are carnivorous plants, so why not carnivorous trees? What can we possibly know, after all, at the age of six? And while the question hadn't occurred to four of the five children, Raphael, the fifth, was getting seriously worried. It was already dark outside the tree, but now it was pitch black, dark enough that you couldn't make out your hand ten centimetres in front of your face. And the smell, and the dampness; we can't know what it's like inside our mother's bellies, but it must have been like this, mustn't it? *Warmer and softer*, Raphael thought, *because this is the belly of a tree that is swallowing us whole, and it's pitch black because the hole we came in through has closed back up.*

'Hugo!' he called, in the soft wood and the blunt splinters.

'Shh!' Hugo responded simply and solemnly, and everyone understood that something was up.

Through the creaking of the wood and the rustling of the leaves caressed by the night breeze, the five children now distinctly heard steps approaching. How could they not hear them? They were impossible to miss. The footfalls of someone or something who was afraid of nothing, who had no qualms about being heard. And against all expectations, voices. But it wasn't Enzo, and it wasn't a wild animal, or a monster: it was the reedy, panicked voices of Yasmine and Emma. Huddled together, touching but not seeing each other, Lilou and Jade thought for a moment that Hugo was going to call out to their friends and offer them help, or maybe invite them to join them in the tree trunk; after all, the girls often played together at school, and they were always invited to each other's birthday parties. The only reason they weren't together tonight was because Emma had waited for Yasmine to pull herself together; otherwise all four of them definitely would have been in the trunk. But Hugo barely thought before making his decision: there wasn't enough room in the tree, even if they squeezed, and the two little girls had never really been his friends, and that was what counted. *Plus*, Hugo thought, *they are heading in the right direction, so they won't get lost.*

So he said nothing; he made no sound, and the others did likewise, or almost, because suddenly a loud gurgle reverberated through the tree trunk.

It's getting ready to digest us! Raphael thought, on the verge of panic, terrified at the idea that the entrance to the trunk had closed back up like a trap and its digestive juices were threatening to seep from the soft walls to carefully dissolve the flesh of all five of them. Yasmine and Emma hadn't noticed the astonishing gastric rumble, and they continued on their way, limping like a single organism, arm in arm, occasionally looking back over their shoulder with a worried glance, drawn by some indeterminate point far ahead, where the forest ended or where only a few metres remained between the trees and civilization, normalcy, safety, basically everything not cut from the cloth of savagery, horror, and blood spilled in the dirt.

'Sorry,' Mathis whispered once the footsteps were far enough away. 'It's my stomach. I'm starving.'

And the incongruous sound resonated again, as if to confirm the truth of his statement. Raphael felt partly relieved. He was still in the dark, the cold, the damp. He had just seen his teacher's skull bashed in by a rock, but, good news, at least they weren't being swallowed alive by a man-eating tree.

'But you're always eating,' Jade whispered, before Hugo's second authoritative 'Shh!' shut them all up.

The children cocked an ear, staying as still and silent as possible, even though their uncomfortable positions sometimes required moving a foot or shifting their weight to the other cheek. It must have been Yasmine and Emma doubling back, Raphael thought, to reassure himself. But squinting to try to make out the approaching dark shadow, Hugo had already figured out that it couldn't be the two little girls. The closer the shape got, the more Hugo recognized the easy gait, the assured step, and the head slightly sunk between the shoulders that made Enzo look like a rugby player or a heavyweight boxer, even though he didn't remotely have the build for it. Once again, a voice rose up in the forest, echoing through the tree trunks, seeming to come from everywhere at once.

'Yasmine! Emma!' shouted the voice, weighed down with all of its owner's hatred and rage. 'I know you're here! I can hear you!'

In the darkness of the supine trunk, the five children shivered, imagining maybe it was them Enzo had heard, the rumbling of Mathis's stomach or the scuff of Jade's foot, which had just moved. What would he do if he found them? Would he be able to hurt them? Hugo was with them, after all, and he was posted at the entrance to the tree trunk. To reach them, Enzo would have to get through him, and everyone in the class knew there had never been an open confrontation between the two boys, two sides of the same coin, yin and yang in the schoolyard, whom nothing could bring together, at risk of compromising the fragile social relations between the groups of little kids. (As for the bigger kids, there were other forces at play, but it is beyond our scope to raise them here.) Hugo was a charismatic role model to many boys and the object of adoration of many little girls, while Enzo was a little kingpin, a terror to be avoided at all costs, whose only friends were self-effacing children who served as his slaves and willing punching bags, imagining that their fate would be much worse if they didn't pretend to idolize their ruthless master. Nathan and Raphael had alternately played this role, as had Milo, a big kid from second grade too stupid to understand that all it would have taken was a smack from him to put Enzo in his place. So Hugo let Enzo have at whomever was in his path and, like a tacit understanding, Enzo never went after the children who gravitated around Hugo, even though the entourage could vary, depending on which way the wind was blowing. However, the unspoken rules governing relations in Fred's little elementary class were hypothetical; did the rules still apply, now that a child had killed an adult? Without an indisputable authority figure, what remained? Would Enzo continue to respect the status quo? Or would he, at the slightest suspicious sound, throw himself on the entrance to the tree trunk to cave in Hugo's skull as he had Fred's? Enzo would attack Hugo, Raphael thought, split him down the middle, gut him, and wade through his organs to grab Jade and Lilou, who would meet the same fate, and eventually reach him, plunge a hand tipped by sharp nails into his chest to rip out his heart and throw it in his face, or devour it, or tear it into a thousand crimson pieces, limp meat, as he imagined his heart must be. It would be the same colour as the offal his mother sometimes brought home from the butcher and fried with a bit of parsley, which melted in your mouth with Saturday mash. *Mommy*, Raphael thought, *I want my mommy*. And he was on the verge of shouting that with all his might, crying and calling out as loudly as he could, but he held back, once again battling the little demon that kept visiting him with increasing insistence and intensity since the bus had closed its folding doors and cut off his mother mid-sentence, so he would never know what she was asking him to not forget, above all. Raphael was trembling and biting the inside of his cheeks, and the sound of Enzo's footsteps crushing the leaves seemed not to retreat, as if he sensed their presence in the tree trunk, as if he were circling them, guided by a predator's sixth sense, or maybe it was just an impression, brought on by terror and the desire to have it all over with as fast as possible, that Enzo go away, that they reach the road and finally go home and forget this whole affair.

'I think he's gone,' Hugo said, after what seemed like an eternity to Raphael and the others.

Trying not to make too much noise, the children dragged themselves out of the trunk, shook and slapped their pyjamas to get rid of the pieces of wood and damp leaves that stuck to them, and, in unison, they turned to Hugo to find out what the plan was. Raphael wanted to shout *Mommy*, Lilou and Jade were exhausted and on the verge of tears, Mathis was starving, his hunger even more acute because he couldn't stop thinking about it, and for the first time since Fred's death, Hugo felt himself vacillate, overcome by the anxiety of not making the right decision, when this time, of all the times, he had to play this role and lead his classmates to the place required in the manner required. This particular time, his decision involved the lives of five children, his own included. *I don't know what we are supposed to do,* he thought. *I'm not an adult. I'm a kid. You're on your own! Leave me out of it! Why are you looking at me like that?* his look seemed to ask, which none of the children could make out in the dark forest. *I can't take care of you. I'm a little kid. It's the adults who know what to do. My mommy, or your mommy, Jade, adults, not kids, you see?* But where were the adults? Fred was dead. And Jade's and Hugo's mommies had left and hadn't come back as planned. There were no more parents. There might not ever be any again. Who was to say?

'We can't head toward the road along the trail,' Hugo said. 'Enzo went that way.'

Lilou let out a sob, as if she suddenly felt authorized to make a sound now that Hugo had confirmed that Enzo was far away.

'I want my mommy,' she stammered between sniffles.

And her cries were echoed, because now Raphael gave in to his sorrow.

'I want my mommy too,' he whined.

And a lump formed in Mathis's throat, as perhaps it finally dawned on him what was going on, and in Jade's throat, as she also started calling for her mother, and, finally, by contagion, because crying begets crying, in the throat of Hugo, who was now crying silent tears. Somewhere, far away, Yasmine and Emma were sobbing too, as were Nathan, and Océane, and Louis, and in the dark forest, in the little perimeter that represented one one-hundredth of the entire wooded area, if you cocked an ear, you could hear a tearful symphony of 'Mommy!' rise above the treetops, whether spoken or simply thought so hard that it had resonated in the sap-filled hearts of the broad, deciduous trees and the towering evergreens. The cries of the children calling for their mothers had filled the space and made everything tremble, tremors that reached the most obtuse of sensibilities, moving anyone who could detect the vibration, that is, anyone other than you, dear reader, who have the privilege and the curse of grasping the unbearable bird's-eye view of a forest, plunged into the darkness of one inconsequential night, from which rise the cries for help of children left to their own devices, and children who have died, or who will die, and whose salvation you can do nothing for. That is your lot, and that is theirs, tragic roles that each will have to play as best they can, until the last page.

III

In the dark of the night, the pond – or it may have been a lake, or an ocean – was like a slick layer of oil, with no waves or lapping, just dotted with greasy rings, which could be liquid impurities, gas, motor oil, or the reflection of far-off galaxies on the still surface of the water. Océane, Nathan, and Louis were standing before this expanse of water as if before a precipice, disconcerted, worried. Since taking off from the camp, they had initially run, and, soon out of breath, they had slowed to a halt. All three of them sat on the ground, listening to ensure they hadn't been followed, both reassured at detecting no trace of Enzo and terrified to discover the sounds, cries, and hundreds of wild murmurs that the belly of the forest produced on its own.

'If you hear a troll, let me know, and I'll take care of it,' Océane said.

'There's no such thing as trolls, Océane,' Nathan said. 'And even if there were, you couldn't kill them.'

'Why not?' Océane sputtered, dismayed.

'Because it's a game. You know it's a game. The troll hunter game.'

'Nonsense,' Océane said. 'There is such a thing as trolls. I've killed one!'

No sooner was the sentence out of her mouth than she believed it. In her memory, she had created the story of the fight, the difficulty she had defeating the abominable creature, its noxious smell, its disgusting buboes that when pierced seeped their curdled pus, all concrete elements of this heroic confrontation, which she was now convinced had taken place. And seeing the conviction in his friend's blue eyes, Nathan had a moment of doubt, prattled on for another moment, said, 'Ah?' and then nothing more, which meant that he believed her, just as she had begun to believe her fairy tale, because, on the damp soil of the Morvan forest, eyes recently filled with the blood and terror spurting from their teacher's shattered skull, anything could be believed. It was believable before, and even more so now. *And yes*, Nathan allowed, *trolls exist, and my friend Océane has killed one, and if I want to survive this night and the monsters that inhabit it and maybe even the nights that follow, I would be better off at her side and I shouldn't annoy her. We're lost, we don't know where, it's dark, it's night, it's cold, animals are prowling, as are things we are too little to have learned the names of, so yes, Océane is a little girl, but she is a little girl who can hunt trolls and, more importantly, who is not scared, who is so strong, confident, and so pretty too, has been so pretty for so long. Why, for so long, has she not understood that I, Nathan, like her and want to hold her in my arms and kiss her and most of all, yes, most of all, I want her to want nothing more than to be near me, for me to be near her, for her to talk to me and want me to talk to her too. So yes, okay, you're right, you must be right, you're the one who decides, Océane, you are the troll hunter, and if you say we go this way, then that's the way we will go.*

And Océane decided, Nathan approved, Louis disapproved of Nathan's decision, Océane approved Louis's disapproval and put the blame on Nathan, Océane made the decision that Louis had implicitly suggested, Nathan submitted to the other two, and the decision to keep walking rather than go back to camp carried.

'Trolls masquerade as trees,' Louis the wolf man said. 'Once they transform, you can't tell the difference between a tree and a troll. They have green moss on their skin, just like trees, and their skin looks like bark, and their hair is like branches with leaves at the end of them, and their blood is cold, so you can walk right up and touch them and you won't feel any heat, and they know how to stay really still, even more still than rocks, but behind their bark-skin eyelids they see you, and with their moss-filled nostrils they smell you, and even if most of the time they are sleeping, sometimes they are also hungry and watching everything going on around them. Sometimes it's a fox or a rabbit or a deer.'

Nathan hadn't wanted to hear any more because he knew that the other little animals that trolls feed on are children lost in the woods, if possible at night, when the shadows of things resemble other shadows of things, so he interrupted him and said, 'Yes, maybe trolls exist, but maybe not in France, maybe in other countries, sure, but here no one ever talks about them, so there can't really be any in this forest, right, Océane? Where did you kill your troll, come to think of it? It wasn't in this forest, was it?'

'Yes,' Océane answered. 'It was here. I remember it well, even that I had come here with my parents for a walk. It was right here, there were the exact same trees, well, I thought they were trees, and I killed the troll over here, near the dirt road.'

Nathan didn't know what to think or believe, like when Christmas was coming, and everything pointed to the fact that Santa Claus didn't exist, when clues were piling up, but his parents and grandparents and uncles and aunts kept talking about reindeer flying through the air and an old guy who could deliver millions of gifts in a single night, when everything, all year long, was depressingly matter-of-fact and made total sense and then suddenly, for one night, magic existed, and he had never really thought about it this way, but what was more likely, when you got right down to it? That magic didn't exist, except for one night a year, or that adults, our own parents no less, all got together to tell children cruel lies? Neither of the two options was acceptable, and for a whole year Nathan didn't know what to believe or think about Christmas. Similarly, on this night, he could not be certain about anything, neither about the shameless lie told by his friend Océane, nor about the presence of hideous, slimy creatures all around him in this dreadful night, disguised as trees, ready to grab him by the arm to stuff him into their fetid mouths and devour his fresh flesh. Around any of the trees, a monster lurking, in any of the shadows draped around them a mortal danger, Enzo or a wolf or something even worse, so without the certainty that would have led to a clear decision, he had gone with the flow, with the direction chosen by his friends – were they truly his friends? – smack through the middle of the monsters and ogres and child-eating beasts, but at least he wouldn't be alone. When no decision can be made, we go along with the decisions of those we trust, and if there is no one to trust, we follow the ones we love. Because maybe, yes, Nathan loved Océane a little more than he was willing to admit when people teased him, and even if she wasn't really a troll hunter, and even if they were just a bunch of terrified children lost in the woods, he preferred to be terrified and lost with her than without her, and maybe be devoured by a troll or have his skull caved in by that lunatic

Enzo, but devoured or crushed or starved or bled to death or poisoned with her rather than without her.

And they had arrived at the pond, or the lake, or whatever this endless expanse of black water was, and the three children stopped and didn't look at one another, because their attention was drawn to the opposite hidden shore. Santa's sleigh had just crashed in front of their eyes, and once again, they had to make an arbitrary decision.

S andra tried calling again, twice, three times, ten times, as many times, she thought, as her battery would allow. If she didn't manage to reach Fred, he and the children would worry, when there was no reason to, no, really, no reason. She was lost, that was all. She would spend the night under a blanket of dead leaves and find her way in the light of dawn. *There is no reason to get upset, all right, Jade? Fred, put my daughter on the phone, please. All right, Jade? There is no reason to worry. Go get into your pyjamas, slip into your sleeping bag, and by the time you wake up, I'll be back, and I'll give you a big kiss to say sorry for having gotten so stupidly lost, okay, Jade? A big kiss to say sorry, sorry, sorry.* That was what Sandra would have liked to have said if someone, good lord, anyone, had answered the damn phone, but the synthesized sound of dispassionate rings, regular and hungry, each one eating away a bit more at the battery's remaining life, now almost dead, *sorry, sorry, sorry, Jade, sorry, sorry, sorry, Mommy, I got away, I ran off, and I followed Hugo because I was afraid. I know I should have stayed in camp and waited for you, Mommy, and you would have made everything better, but I was afraid, so afraid, Mommy, Mommy, I want my mommy!* Jade was crying, crouching against a tree. It hadn't even occurred to her friends to tell her to be quiet; they were all consumed by the same emotion as soon as she had said the magic word, *Mommy*, which generates in every human being, in every era and every country, a simultaneous shiver of comfort and absence. And it was as if, before, during, or after the rings sounded, Sandra had heard the cries and calls for help, or was it simply her imagination playing tricks on her and transforming every sound in the woods and the

{ 76 }

night – the creaking and screeching – into the distant moans of children, her child in particular, that she was suffering so much at the thought of having abandoned, even though it wasn't willingly? Which direction did it come from, that cry of distress she thought she had heard? From the right? The left? Straight ahead? Behind her? Now that the phone had gone dead, her battery run down from the repeated calls, and her ear was free to hear all the noises around her, had she really heard shouting? From over there, maybe. *But come on, don't be silly, the children are in bed and Fred will have come up with a story to reassure them, a credible explanation so that Jade would drift peacefully off to sleep, so why keep walking in the direction of cries that probably don't exist? Why not instead sit down, lie down, go to sleep, and make tomorrow come as quickly as possible, with the happy ending that will come with the daylight?*

'Yes, it will be better in the daylight, so why should I go now?' Océane said. 'You can't even see the other side. It could be a giant lake, or the sea. We don't know. And how do you swim across the sea?'

'No, really. It would be better to stop and sleep here,' Hugo said, standing near the tree trunk. 'We'll reach the road tomorrow. It would be better to hide in the tree and wait for tomorrow.'

'But why wait for tomorrow?' Louis asked Océane. 'Enzo is after us. If he finds us, he's going to kill us, just like he did Fred. He'll split our heads open with a rock. You have to get help. It won't be that hard. You swim and keep an eye on the shore of the lake. There are always houses with people in them around lakes. You can even see them at night, because they turn on the lights in their houses on the lake, so as soon as you see a light, you swim toward it, and you knock on the door and tell them what happened and then you will have saved us all, Océane, because you are the only one who knows how to swim. The only one.'

'Because there are no adults left, not one, so we have to find some, do you hear me?' Emma said to Yasmine, who had just stopped and plopped down on her bum, crying, for the thousandth time. 'We have to find the road, a car will go by, and we'll wave it down, and we will be rescued and all the others will be rescued too, and we'll go home. Get up, please, get up. We can't stop. He's going to catch up to us. Listen. I can hear him over that way.'

'Yasmine! Emma!' Enzo yelled in the wooded night. 'Yasmine! Emma!' his voice tinged with mischief and cruelty. 'Emma! Yasmine!' Enzo laughed, walking calmly, as if certain he would eventually catch up with the little girls, as if there were no other possible outcome that day, now that he had eliminated Fred and taken over.

No one would tell him to shut up anymore, and no one would punish him anymore, and no one would tell him to go to bed, or to clean his plate, Enzo thought. And if he liked the idea of taking revenge on the two little pests by beating them with all his might with whatever he could find, then no one would stop him. No one would stop him from doing anything now, he thought, heading west, not even knowing it was west, but since Yasmine's cries could be heard for miles around, he would have to be a pretty pathetic hunter to let that sort of prey get away. It would be easy with her, and her friend, and then he didn't really know what he would do, but he was delighted at all the options available to him; he could hunt down all of the imbeciles and crush their heads one by one, or he could reach the road and flag down a car and go home to take care of his father, doing the same thing to him that he did to Fred, because, if there was anyone in the world that Enzo hated or feared more than Fred and his stupid punishments, it was his father, his incomprehensible shouting, his punches and kicks that landed without Enzo knowing why, his insults, his humiliations, his hateful habit of treating his son like an imbecile, a weakling, a good-for-nothing. He might finally change his mind with a rock sunk into his skull, and maybe in looking inside his open head, Enzo would understand what was wrong with him. Would his blood be as red as Fred's? And would his brain be greyish or bright white streaked with fine scarlet veins, like the brains he had seen in the display in the meat department at the supermarket? There must be something wrong in his father's head, in the heads of everyone who spent their time chewing him out and preventing him from living his life.

'Yasmine! Emma! And the rest of you!' Enzo yelled. 'Do you hear me? Does everyone hear me?'

Even though no one answered, plenty of children distinctly heard their classmate's terrifying voice. For Sandra, who was far away, it was just a faint echo bouncing off the rocks and the tree trunks, but for Hugo, Jade, Mathis, Lilou, and Raphael, who had decided to stay close to the tree trunk that was their refuge, the words resonated too loudly for their liking.

'Time for bed, children,' Enzo went on. 'I'm going to tell you a story so that you have sweet dreams.'

'No, I don't want to. I'm scared,' Océane said to Louis.

'We're scared too,' Louis said. 'But we can't do anything about that. You're the only one who can save us, right, Nathan?'

It was the first time Louis needed Nathan's approval, and it took Nathan by such surprise that he agreed without thinking.

'But if I don't find anyone,' Océane asked, 'what will I do all alone on the other side of the lake?'

'Well, you'll rest a little and then you'll come back, and we'll find another solution,' Louis said.

'If she doesn't want to, it's okay,' Nathan said.

But Océane didn't care about his opinion and kept staring at Louis in the hopes that he would change his mind, because it was him and him alone she didn't want to disappoint, and she knew that despite the cold, despite the night, despite the fear, if Louis asked her to swim across the lake, she would have no choice but to do it, as absurd as the child's decision was, and she may even have been aware of the absurdity, and the madness, but she was in love, head over heels in love the way you are at age six, without knowing that this love would be as fleeting as it was powerful, and as powerful as it was secret, and misunderstood, an attachment, an obsession that Océane had never called, nor would ever call, 'love,' just as Nathan would never manage to name that endless frustration combined with the constant need to get Océane's attention, to do whatever he could, whenever he could, without even realizing it, to make her interested in him, even if only for an instant, and then another, as long as was possible.

'Once upon a time,' Enzo yelled, just as Océane, who couldn't hear him, was pulling down her pyjamas, which were covered with brave, obedient little mice who all wanted to fly through the skies like the birds.

Yasmine sobbed noisily, from exhaustion as much as fear.

'Run!' Emma said. 'He's right there!'

The two friends started running again even faster, scratched by branches, tripping over the exposed roots on the ground, but not stopping, their faces contorted with effort and crying, running straight ahead, to where they thought they would reach the road, which couldn't be much farther now.

'The mice did their homework,' Enzo went on, 'and they answered all the nice teacher's questions, and they knew that if they worked hard and were obedient, they could fly like birds.'

Hugo drew closer to his companions and whispered, 'Let's get back in the tree,' mouthing the words carefully so that the others would be able to read his lips. Everyone agreed.

'Do you know the story?' Enzo asked, as Océane, dressed only in her underwear and pyjama top, like Hello Kitty, was stepping into the water and feeling the slimy softness of the silt underfoot.

'Yasmine! Emma! You're good little mice, aren't you?'

But breathless, their lungs on fire, their thigh muscles gnawed at by lactic acid, Yasmine and Emma couldn't have answered, even if they could hear him.

'But it was a special class,' Enzo added, 'a class of mice that also had a beautiful eagle in it. Not an ugly, old seagull, but a beautiful, majestic eagle, with a white head and a yellow beak.'

'It's not so bad once you get in,' Océane said, 'but it's still cold.'

'You're the best, Océane,' Nathan said.

'We'll wait right here. We won't go anywhere,' Louis said.

To the sounds of the forest were added the sound of the little girl's feet slapping on the water, a little girl who knew how to swim, but not well enough to do it in silence, so from time to time, a noisy splash rippled through the cold air when her feet would inadvertently come out of the water because of an awkward movement and land with a slap like a frightened carp darting away.

'Are you okay?' Nathan asked, every time he heard the sound.

'Yes,' Océane would answer, each time sounding farther away and more out of breath.

'Stop talking to her,' Louis ordered. 'You're tiring her out.'

And so the two children were quiet, listening to the irregular splashes created by their friend on the black mirror surface.

'But, you know, the eagle,' Enzo cackled, 'he didn't give a hoot about working hard to learn to fly. The eagle had been flying since he was little. The eagle didn't have a choice, did he? When you have to jump out of the nest, either you fly, or you crash at the foot of the mountain. The eagle has to fly, otherwise he's not a real eagle, you see? No, you don't see, because you are all little mice! All of you, do you hear me? And do you know what eagles eat?'

'There,' Emma said to Yasmine, panting, pointing straight ahead, to an area where the forest seemed less dense and where, no, they weren't dreaming it, light seemed to dance on the tree trunks.

'I'm tired,' Océane said, swallowing water in the middle of her sentence.

The little girl paddled as best she could, but in the dark she had a hard time remembering which side was the shore she thought she had been swimming parallel to.

'Louis!' she called out a bit louder, at the risk of swallowing some of the black water.

'Did you hear that?' Nathan asked.

'What?' Louis said.

'Océane, she's calling you.'

They both cocked their ear, and from a distance, a long way off on the lake, the little voice reached them again.

'Louis!'

'We're here!' Louis cried.

'I can't keep going,' Océane spluttered, this time loud enough for her friends to hear.

She was fighting to stay afloat, fighting the pains in her thighs and her arms, which were becoming increasingly acute as she moved, but she had no choice other than to keep kicking her feet and moving her arms, in what was originally a breast stroke, not of the classic variety, but a breast stroke that had now changed into chaotic writhing to keep her head above water, to survive.

'Something's wrong. We have to help her,' Nathan said, throwing himself into the water. 'Océane!' he cried.

'I'm over here!' she managed to respond, marshalling her last strength to head toward the voice, a point of reference that she could follow to get back to terra ferma.

'Océane!' Nathan cried again, his feet sinking into the silt, water up to his knees, wetting the bottom of his pyjamas, which he felt sticking to his skin. 'We're over here! Come back!'

I'm trying! the little girl settled for just thinking, gripped by the pain, consumed by the burning in her chest.

'Océane! Are you okay?' yelled Louis, who had stayed on shore.

I'll be okay now, I'll be okay, Emma thought, realizing that the light that was sweeping the tree trunks a few metres ahead of them was the headlights of a vehicle on the winding road.

So when Yasmine took a break to catch her breath and vomit a little of the sandwich she had eaten before the evening around the campfire, Emma grabbed her by the arm and pulled her until she started running again. They were so close to the goal now, they couldn't stop. They had to run, and run some more, until they were both safe, because the truck – they could hear that it was a truck now – could go right past before they reached the roadside, and how much longer would they have to wait for another vehicle to pass this way?

'Eagles eat little mice!' yelled Enzo, flushed with anger.

He yelled so loud that he didn't hear the dull thud Yasmine's and Emma's bodies made when the semi-trailer hit them, sending them flying onto the roadside, one of them landing in a large thicket of ferns and the other in a field of nettles. The driver didn't find them when he looked around with his flashlight, thinking he had hit a small deer, a fox, or a young wild boar. Disappointed he wouldn't be bringing any game home, but reassured that the collision hadn't damaged his truck, the driver wiped the traces of blood from his bumper and radiator grille and got back on the road with a shrug.

When Enzo found the road two minutes later, the truck was already a long way off.

'Océane!' Nathan cried.

'Océane!' Louis cried.

The two boys couldn't hear their friend anymore, not her voice or even the splashing they had been able to make out just two minutes earlier, but that had given way to the terrible silence of water that no wind stirred. Nathan and Louis shouted, and shouted, even more fervently because they realized what had happened. They shouted to prolong the moment when they were both pretending to have hope, as if the sound of the desperate splashing of their friend's arms and legs as she drowned hadn't reached them, as if her little voice, filled with water and tears, had not called out 'Mommy' a few metres in front of them, just a few metres, but still too far for them to come to her aid. They shouted to try to shed as much of their responsibility for the tragedy as they could, shouted to externalize the guilt that filled them. Louis was the first to stop shouting. He turned his back on the lake and started moving, as if sleep-walking, toward the forest. It was like a signal, like the solemn declaration of a doctor calling the time of death when nothing more can be done with any decency, and Nathan felt rise up in him all the hatred, resentment, and jealousy that had been building up over all the months he had been relegated to his role of underling, stable boy, domestic, while Louis, in every scenario he had imagined, systematically got the good role, the role of the prince, the magician, or the wolf man. But the worst thing was that it was Louis who had forced Océane to swim, and now that their friend was resting in her bed of black silt, that could only mean one thing.

'You killed her!' Nathan shouted, hurling himself on Louis after a short, lightning-quick sprint.

The collision sent both boys tumbling, Louis absorbing his classmate's weight and velocity with his chest as he made contact with the ground, instantly winding him. Straddling him, Nathan was able to unleash his rage without any resistance. He pummelled Louis with his fists, grabbed his friend's head with both hands, shook it and knocked it against the large root of a willow tree. In about ten seconds – which was an eternity in a child's fight – Louis's face was swollen and bloody. Ten seconds after that, he was unconscious; the impact with the root had essentially split open the back of his skull. His heart stopped beating in the next ten seconds, as Nathan's blows grew weaker, and it slowly dawned on him what he was doing and what he had done. Out of breath, his hands bloody, the bottom of his pyjamas wet, Nathan's horrified eyes grew wide as he took in Louis's face and his worrisome stillness.

'Louis?' he asked, gently shaking his friend. 'Oh no,' he said in a low voice, as his face turned purple, and he started to bawl. 'Oh no,' he repeated, standing up, looking around him, and realizing just how alone he was and how alone he would always be now that his two best friends were gone. 'Oh no,' he moaned again 'No, no, no, no,' he intoned, sobbing. 'No, no, no, no,' he repeated, as he started to walk toward the trees, and then run, and then run faster, crying, his mind blank, still droning 'no' like a hiccup caught in his throat, tears in his eyes, tears on his cheeks, tears in his lungs. 'No, no, no,' he continued, as if it were the only word he could utter, the complete and final negation of everything, running even faster, so he would no longer have to see the horrors, no more stories, no more trolls, no more wolf men, no! *I want to go home! I want my mommy! I don't want to play this game anymore! No, no, no! Mommy, my mommy, I want my…* Then an evergreen branch stopped Nathan's litany and his running in their tracks, ripping part of the skin from his face. Thrown off balance, propelled by his momentum, he couldn't prevent his fall and tumbled to the ground, landing on his shoulder.

A few seconds elapsed before Nathan could collect himself, dazed by his run-in with the branch. When he tried to get up, he felt a terrible pain pierce his spine. A cry shot out from the back of his little throat. It took him a few minutes to risk moving again and to try to identify his injuries, but now that he was stuck on the ground, his broken legs wrapped around each other like the legs of a puppet, he would have all the time he needed to assess their seriousness, their irreversibility, and the consequences for the night, which promised to be very long. Once again, between the century-old tree trunks, the nocturnal fauna heard a cry ring out, made by a small human, the wunderkind of the animal kingdom, master of fire and metal, but just as fragile when it collided with the laws of physics and the cosmos.

IV

The sun had come up, revealing a cloak of damp fog that had risen from the ground and gotten tangled in the trunks and the branches, gently cooling them to let them know that a new day had arrived, filled with the quiet savagery so typical of natural spaces, where plants try to develop faster than animals can consume them, and where animals try to draw on the plants' energy to avoid the fangs of their brethren for one more day. Except for Enzo, who was still sleeping, all those whom this tale has so far spared had seen the sky grow paler, and then the first rays appeared on the horizon, because their sleep had been light, punctuated by fretful wakefulness, stifled sobs, startled awakenings that dragged them out of nightmares in which trees, beasts, and monsters grabbed them to bring their travels to an end. Like a litter of bunnies emerging from a burrow, Hugo, Lilou, Mathis, Jade, and Raphael exited the old log, one by one, in the light of day discovering surroundings they thought would be familiar.

'Where are we?' Mathis asked Hugo, who was scanning the area, looking worried.

'The dirt road shouldn't be far,' Jade said.

'We were wrong,' Hugo confirmed. 'The dirt road we took wasn't the same one the bus did. I don't know where we are.'

And before his friends could panic, he added, 'But if we follow the dirt road in the other direction, we'll arrive back at camp.'

'I don't want to go back to camp,' Lilou said, staring into the distance.

The little girl was trembling, her arms crossed against her torso, her mouth distorted in permanent sadness. When she closed her eyes, over and over she saw Fred's blood spattering by the campfire. So she hadn't been able to sleep, hadn't even wanted to, huddled in the body heat of her slumbering classmates, but had stayed fully awake, eyes wide open to the dank darkness of the log. She couldn't get the horrific episode she had witnessed out of her mind, or understand it, or learn the slightest lesson from it. An adult, the only adult who was supposed to take care of her, had been killed, obliterated, destroyed, and this initial trauma reverberated in her, and its power destroyed every part of her budding personality. Dolls, princesses, sparkly dresses, pink strollers, a plastic stove, the 'my darlings,' the 'my loves,' life as she knew it, all the carefully constructed images of her future, assembled in miniature in her bedroom like a seed, like a fetus, that would grow, the stove becoming a real stove, the stroller a real stroller, and the dolly in it a real baby, on this stage, in this scale model that was the beginning and the end of her existence, none of it featured a smashed skull or spurting blood, and that was as it should be, but for Lilou, this posed a metaphysical problem. The event had infiltrated her, like a pebble in the gears, like a semicolon in a line of computer code, and she had crashed; she simply stopped functioning, her mind at least, her ability to think, her manner of perceiving the world. Nothing was working anymore, which was, to some extent, the case for all the children who had witnessed Fred's murder, but in Lilou it took on psychiatric proportions.

'I don't want to go back to camp,' she repeated, her eyes darting around, her features still dark, like a robot, like a crazy person, her friends thought.

'I'm starving,' said Mathis, whose stomach had been plaguing him since he'd opened his eyes.

'Me too,' Jade said.

'Me too,' Raphael said.

'Me too,' Hugo said. 'We need to eat.'

'But the food is back at camp,' Raphael said. 'And I don't want to go there either. I bet Enzo is there. He must be hungry too.'

'I can go get food, and you can wait here,' Hugo suggested.

'No,' Jade said. 'We have to stay together. What will we do if you don't come back?'

'Then we have to find the road,' Hugo concluded. 'We can't stay here and just wait. It's possible no one knows what happened, and they won't come get us if we don't let them know.'

'No one, no one,' Lilou repeated, sobbing.

At these words, Raphael was gripped with fear. A lot of things had scared him during the evening and the night, but it hadn't occurred to him that, in fact, it was possible that no one would be coming to get them. All night, struggling in an exhausting half-slumber, he had wished with all his might for the sun to come up. He even dreamed about it, crying with joy when his cruel dream showed him the warm, heavenly, yellow body pierce through the trees, but now that day had broken, nothing had changed, no one had rescued them, and the possibility that that was how it would be the whole day, and the whole night, and all the other days, and all the other nights, had started to eat away at him right there, in his chest, at that blue place where tears are born and hope dies. So this is what it was like to be abandoned in the woods, like Hop o' My Thumb and his brothers, like Hansel and Gretel, lost in the dark forest where wild animals live, where chasms open up under your feet, where a child-eating witch may well have built her house. Who was to say? Anything was possible, anything, thought Raphael, who had also remembered the game Océane and Louis and Nathan played, the troll game. I mean, why not? Trolls masquerading as trees, trolls masquerading as boulders, and also creatures, animals, plants. There was so much he didn't know, so many surprising, marvellous, and terrible things that he discovered each day, often on television, so many things whose existence he never would have suspected that were in fact real, so in the cold, the hunger, and the pallor of the morning, reality struggled to impose itself with the weight of other mornings, and along with the feeling of not experiencing what he was experiencing – or of experiencing it in a totally different way than on other days – Raphael felt the ball of terror in him swell and radiate through his body, making his hands tremble, making the hair on the back of his neck stand on end, but it also melted and ran down over his eyes, which no longer knew what they were seeing: a grove or a buffalo? A creeper of ivy or a viper? And as the little party started walking, he even doubted that his companions were there at all, with him, at his side, weary ghosts with hesitant movements and hushed voices. Enzo might have found them and killed them all in their sleep, everyone except him, or including him. What would it change? Who was to say what you see or feel and how you walk when you are dead? Maybe exactly like this.

After a long night's sleep spent in the shelter of one of the tents in camp, Enzo rose naked. The night before, slimy and sticky, he had decided to take off his pyjamas, which were soaked in Fred's blood, and just slide into the fluffy sleeping bag, where he instantly fell asleep.

The sun seemed to be up, and the grey light was the light of a morning at the start of the school year. Enzo took a few steps on the soft ground of the shelter, before stopping, lifting his head like a hunting dog, and starting to rapidly sniff. A smell was following him, a heady, metallic smell. It wasn't the stink of Fred's dead flesh. That was a smell that Enzo was familiar with, having often been exposed to it when he happened to pass the body of a cat or a hedgehog on his daily walks. This was something else, a delicate bouquet, a note of spice mixed with the pungency of sweat. Was it coming from him? Enzo looked at his hands. They were covered with brown crust up to his forearms. He brought them to his nose, closed his eyes, and took a deeper breath. The smell was persistent, powerful, but he wouldn't have said it was unpleasant. He opened his eyes again and looked at the rest of his body. Blood and grime covered his thighs, his shins, and of course his bare feet, which were showing not a single patch of clean skin, so much had he walked in the dirt. Realizing that his face must also have traces of his crime, he slowly stroked his cheeks and scratched off a bit of the solid film that covered them. He spent a long time looking at the tips of his nails without being able to identify whether they were covered in soil or dried blood. It was only once he was engaged in his morning ablutions at the water tank that he was able to differentiate the substance sticking to him that changed into a reddish fluid from the substance that crumbled into small black particles: one was blood, the other was earth. On his legs, arms, and face, he noticed clear rivulets grow soiled with one or the other. Was this what he was made of? Earth and blood? Dirt and hemoglobin? As if hypnotized, his mind in flight, he spent almost a minute watching the water run down him and mix with Fred's blood and the forest's mud, landing in a drab puddle on the ground, splashing his feet, his puny body gradually turning white again. Sometimes children like to lose themselves in the contemplation of simple things.

Relatively clean, his thirst quenched, Enzo put on his Bermuda shorts and T-shirt and set off in search of food. In a shed at the camp, he discovered the reserves for the weekend, but there was only fruit, chips, and rice, along with loads of unappetizing savoury goods. He wanted sweets for breakfast. He left the shed open and launched an assault on his classmates' backpacks, which their doting mothers had stuffed with chocolate bars, candies, and cookies. Now, that was more like it.

Sitting on a log, stirring up the still-hot ashes of the campfire with a branch, he devoured a package of cookies while listening to the birds chirping. Then he stuffed a bunch of granola bars into his bag and headed north, where he knew some of his classmates had fled. He slid into his belt a small, sharp knife he found in another bag, maybe Sandra's, and in his back pocket he could feel the weight of Fred's cellphone, which he didn't yet know what to do with. What if he called for help? The number for the fire station was 18, if memory served. He could go home and put an end to all this.

No, he thought. Why stop now? He would go all the way. Anyway, all of those imbeciles would tell on him for what he had done to Fred, and he would be punished again. It would be better to take care of them first, to be sure they wouldn't make a fuss, and then call for help, so the only story the adults would hear would be his own.

Enzo remembered what his father would say when he left to go hunting, early on Sunday mornings. It was before the sun was even up, but he wouldn't have missed the spectacle for anything in the world, a huge man dressed in khaki, a broken shotgun in the crook of his arm, sporting a row of bright red cartridges across his chest, laughing, and saying, 'We may not be smarter than pigs, but we're more patient. That's why they end up in paté, and we don't.' *Pigs* was what he called boars, and he often came home with one, sometimes the whole thing, or just a piece when he knew the freezer was full and he preferred to share it with his hunting buddy rather than waste the meat.

'I may not be smarter than pigs,' Enzo repeated to himself, 'but I'm more patient.'

And from that point on, he started walking differently, talking less, being stealthier, cocking his ear at the slightest noise, because now he was no longer playing wolf, as he had done with Yasmine and Emma – how had those two ninnies gotten away? – to scare them rather than to actually catch them. Now he was hunting, and that quiet moan, that tiny squeal that was reaching his ears with increasing clarity as he headed north – he was starting to think that it could be his first prey.

The potter wasp is a member of the *Eumeninae* family, a name naturalists no doubt chose after being horrified by the insect's practices; like most solitary wasps, it had developed a way to feed its young that human beings, with our unfortunate habit of comparing everything to ourselves, would have judged as terribly cruel.

When it lays its sole egg, the potter wasp builds a cone-shaped nest in the ground with its saliva. It places the egg at the bottom of this nest, then it sets off to hunt for caterpillars, which it brings back to the nest to trap alive. When the egg hatches, the larva has an abundant store of fresh meat that it will feed on as it grows, eating the trapped caterpillars alive one by one. Other species of solitary wasps prefer spiders to caterpillars, carefully amputating their legs before delivering them alive to their larva.

When people observe the potter wasp catching its prey, they are struck by its method, the precision of its gestures, the swift, assured way it pounces on the caterpillar, paralyzing it with the venom in its dart, then grabbing it to transport it as best it can. The potter wasp doesn't ask questions. It isn't plagued by doubt. It follows its nature, without emotion or hesitation. And without mercy, of course.

Nathan had spent a few hours shouting, calling for his mother, or anyone who might miraculously have been passing that way in the middle of the night. His cries became more intermittent, weaker, and the piercing pain had deprived him of language, periodically of consciousness too. He passed out for a few minutes, overcome by suffering, but inevitably came to to the sound of a hoarse groan emerging from his throat, which was hard to believe came from such a small body. When dawn broke, he didn't know it, his eyes closed tight on the disappointment of being alive, and when Enzo crept toward him, he wasn't even able to imagine that the person who had finally discovered him could be his saviour. He didn't move, his monotone groaning did not change for a second, and of course he didn't answer when Enzo asked him, laughing, if he had taken up dancing.

'On second thought,' he added, 'I don't think I want you to teach me.'

Enzo crouched near Nathan's face and tried to make out any words in the grim rattle coming out of his classmate's mouth. But he could decipher nothing: no call for help, no invectives, just a noisy, regular exhale. He got up, took out his knife, walked around the child once, cocked his head as if wondering how to go about it, walked around him again, scratched his chin with the tip of the knife, abruptly crouched down again, straddled Nathan like a tiny mount, tossed his weapon aside so he would have both hands free, firmly grabbed his victim's head, turned it so that he was facing the soft carpet of dead leaves, moss, vomit, and mud, and brought all of his weight down on the back of his skull, arms fully extended, until the spasms of the child who was living his last moments stopped for good. Nathan didn't struggle, or only his nervous system did, with no real decision being made, like a hand automatically pulling away from a flame that is burning it. Moving was so painful. More than the pain caused by his skull being pressed against the ground. Suffocating wasn't so painful after all. Almost soothing compared with what he had just endured, when the chill of the night provoked intermittent, uncontrollable shivers, shivers that shook his broken bones, electrifying his body to the point of making him vomit with the pain.

On the verge of death, a few seconds from the end, up to his last moment, Nathan hadn't thought of Océane, or his mother, or anything else for that matter. He thought of nothing. He died thinking of nothing.

The children hadn't found the main road. They hadn't found the dirt road either, the one that led to the camp, or any other dirt road for that matter, nor any dwelling or sign that would have told them whether they were headed in the right direction, whether they were approaching civilization or heading farther into the wild, where the animals reigned, some of which had never seen, and would never see, a human being. No landmarks, no plan, no idea, just intuition that turned out to be faulty, the glaring dissipation of which now set Hugo, Jade, Raphael, Mathis, and Lilou on an erratic trajectory paved with apprehension and a growing, gnawing, persistent worry. None of them were older than seven, so how could they make the right decisions? How could they remember important information, stay calm, and respond wisely? *We're just kids!* Hugo cried, in silence. *There is no one left to help us, and we're scared!*

All the children were thinking the same thing, but none of them said it out loud. Where adults would have torn each other limb from limb looking for someone to blame, the children grew quiet with sadness. *We are all children,* they thought, *and none of us is equipped to deal with such an adversary. We go through life under other people's protection. We listen to instructions and try to follow them. We don't know what's true and what's not. What's fair and unfair. Our world is small. Our world is narrow. We do as we're told. We know we aren't big enough to think for ourselves or make our own choices. We walk along clear paths, we call out for kilometres around, we listen for an answer that never comes. We are alone. Why have you left us alone? Why must we always be alone? Is there no history? No experience? Is there no one we can trust who wields their past like metal stuck to their skin to protect them from what will inevitably happen, and who can tell us and show us how to do likewise? How can we bend the sheet metal and slap it against our forms and perhaps avoid, or at least absorb part of, life's next blow to the ribs? Is there no way to do that? Where are the adults? Where are the elders? The old people gathered around the tree, the camp-fire storytellers who deliberately hide the answers to future riddles in their fables? No one is telling any stories, and cries pierce the silence, offering no other information, cries of terror and screams of pain, rather than legends and their shimmer of ambiguity that would have guided our steps along the black trails carpeted with rotting leaves and needles. But no edifying story comes to our minds, and in looking for a tale to help us find our way, we find only ogres, witches, wolves and, worse still, parents who brought us here to abandon us. All of these stories, all of these tales, repeat ad nauseam that a child has no business alone in the middle of the woods, that no good can come of heading off-road. And yet here we are. No legend, no story, no myth to tell us what children should do if they ever have the misfortune of finding themselves here. If such a story exists, no one's ever told it to us. Birds have eaten the crumbs, and this is where we find ourselves. With no clues, no road, no camp, no sign, arrow, or map, in the twists and turns of a winding labyrinth, made of wind and wandering, we are here, with no hope of soon finding ourselves somewhere else or brutally and abruptly nowhere, and living simultaneously in the terror of being here and of no longer being, for good, a fear that burns almost as much as the hunger that grips our insides and that makes us say, 'Hugo, please, Hugo, we are so hungry, and we want to stop to eat, look around, and kick up some leaves to find blackberries, or wild strawberries or bilberries or bananas, maybe, who knows?' Who among us knows what grows here or where things grow, so, bananas, why not? It would be a surprise, of course, but having arrived at this juncture where anything, even the worst things, seems possible, why not?*

'Oh, okay,' Hugo said. 'Yes, of course, we can stop and look for fruit to eat, but be careful, because mushrooms can be poison and people sometimes die eating fruit they don't recognize, so don't touch any fruit you don't recognize and whatever you do, don't eat it.'

No one dared say that none of them were acquainted with or had ever eaten any wild fruit, or berries, or seeds, because they were too hungry and too ashamed and too everything. 'Because,' quite simply 'because,' plain, raw silence, the docile approval, there you have it, 'because,' because I want my mommy, because I want to go home, because I don't have the strength to think anymore, or the desire to lie, because.

So the children stopped. They scattered like a drop of oil in water, backs bent and eyes squinting, looking at their feet for anything that resembled the colourful fruit they occasionally came upon in the produce section of the supermarket, which they walked through at their parents' sides – their mother's, yes, their mother's, Mommy is the one who does the shopping – as their thoughts turned to the toy department and they didn't care about the rest, the bread, fish, potatoes, batteries, sugar, and dish soap, we have dish soap. Are you sure? 'There, there are some berries, right here, over here!' Raphael spotted them first, the appetizing little red clusters dangling from the pretty green shrub set in the black soil, so vivid against the dark forest floor.

'Look! Look! Over here!' Raphael yelled, and the children gathered around the little tree.

'Are you sure we can eat them?' Jade asked.

'Of course. They look like bilberries,' Raphael answered.

'They look like red currants,' Mathis added, already salivating.

'I've never seen them before,' Hugo said. 'We shouldn't touch them.'

But Mathis's stomach, which had been rumbling for hours, left him little choice, and the boy threw himself on the plant, commonly called February daphne, the botanical name of which is *Daphne mezereum*. It was neither common nor rare to find it in the Burgundian undergrowth, exquisitely in bloom with slim violet petals at the end of the winter, then covered with orangey-red fruit until the summer.

Jade approached Hugo, who was fretting and motionless, while Lilou, Raphael, and Mathis grabbed handfuls of red berries and stuffed them into their mouths, chewing and smiling a smile sometimes twisted by the sourness of the fruit.

'You shouldn't eat that,' Hugo said.

But they were so hungry, and it was just fruit, like the fruit the foxes and the Smurfs eat. It wasn't white-spotted mushrooms, harmful amanitas; it was fruit, and at worst they would get sick and so what? At least they would have eaten because they were hungry, and do you actually know, Hugo, whether or not the plant is safe?

'No, I don't know,' Hugo said.

'So you see,' Mathis concluded, shovelling February daphne berries into his mouth, 'you see, you don't know and I'm hungry.'

He kept gobbling them up like a deranged person, as did Lilou and Raphael, and the three children squealed in satisfaction as they greedily swallowed the appetizing red fruit of the *Daphne mezereum*, the juicy, tasty, terribly toxic fruit of the *Daphne mezereum*.

E ven though the battery on Sandra's phone had been dead for hours, she couldn't help herself, walking a bit at random along the identical-looking trails and, without thinking, reaching into her pocket to try to see the time on the dead device, then, remembering that there was no way to get help or news of her daughter now, thought better of it. Why hadn't Fred answered? What had prevented him? The phone was working – Sandra had distinctly heard the rings sound one by one – so what had happened? Had the teacher forgotten his cellphone at the bottom of a bag, buried so deep that the sound of the muffled ring tones hadn't reached his ears or one of the children's ears? Of course, that was impossible. She hadn't come back all night; Fred would have been worried and answered his phone, even tried to reach her. There must be another explanation, a scenario that wasn't dire, a technical glitch with her phone, for instance. It was plausible. Otherwise, how would you explain that her calls to her husband and those made in desperation to Nathalie had also been lost in the cold indifference of voice mail? Obviously, the problem must be on her end, her phone, a stupid setting that she must not have activated or a complicated feature that she had activated accidentally. It wouldn't be the first time an electronic device had tripped her up. Remote controls, computers, tablets, stereos, car radios – she didn't understand why these devices required such complicated procedures for simple tasks. She remembered as a little girl she would turn on her father's transistor radio by rotating a single volume knob, which also turned the radio off when turned in the opposite direction. Now she railed against all the sophisticated gadgets from which she asked no more than before: her transistor to receive radio programming, her washing machine to wash her clothes, her television to bring her her shows, and her phone, quite simply, to work. But nothing was simple anymore, and she kept finding herself asking her six-year-old daughter to explain how to get a satellite TV decoder or an ADSL modem to work. She had always had a hard time with such things, looking like an old fart to her own daughter, but now Sandra clung to her notorious incompetence with new technology like a lifeline, because that meant she could keep the hope alive that she simply didn't know how to use her phone and that at the other end of her increasingly desperate calls, Fred was fine, Jade was fine, the other children were fine, and Nathalie and her husband were fine too.

'Jade!' she started to shout intermittently left and right as she walked. 'Fred! Jade! Can you hear me?'

How long had the sun been up? How can you tell without a watch or a phone? Sandra felt like she had been walking for hours, but she wasn't used to walking for this long, so it might have been just an impression. The only thing she was sure of was that the sun hadn't yet reached its zenith, and, while that was the only thing she knew about orientation in the outdoors, that meant it wasn't yet noon. But her thighs were aching, the soles of her feet too, despite the running shoes she bought for the occasion. Her stomach was also starting to rumble. *Exercise, a diet, that's what my doctor told me I needed,* she tried joking to herself, but couldn't quite wipe from her face the mask of fatigue and worry that was becoming more deeply etched.

'Jade! Fred!' she yelled, careful that her shouting not betray the flashes of panic that were increasingly seizing her.

Occasionally, sobs rose up in her throat, getting caught for a few seconds, and winded up seeping from her watering eyes. When that happened, she would stop walking, stop shouting, and wait until she had pulled herself together so she could continue on her way and call for help some more.

A few hundred metres behind her, doing everything he could to remain silent and invisible, Enzo slipped easily between the trunks, brambles, and ferns, following this strange woman and her maternal cries at a distance. As long as he was enjoying the ambiguity – was she calling for help or offering it? – the boy didn't make his presence known, preferring to walk as well, perhaps to wear himself out, and keep the illusion alive as long as possible that somewhere, someone needed him and that, paradoxically, at the same time, somewhere, someone was waiting for him if he needed them.

It started with a stomach ache. Their tongues had been burning for a while, but sometimes that happened after eating fruit at the cafeteria: grapefruit, kiwi, oranges, and pineapple can sting your tongue and your lips. It happens, so there was no point in worrying about it, but then, in their stomachs, a pain squeezing like a hand twisting what's inside. The children started walking again, with Hugo and Jade in front, Raphael, Mathis, and Lilou a few metres behind, already with an upset tummy, as their mothers would say, not feeling themselves, as they would sometimes say as well, already weaker and clutching their stomachs.

'Can you slow down?' Raphael said.

'But we're not walking fast,' Hugo answered.

The two leaders took a breather to let the stragglers catch up, then started off with renewed vigour, because while Hugo and Jade may have been walking a little fast, they were so hungry, their stomachs gnawed at by other forces, and there was no way they were going to go through another night without being fed. It was out of the question.

'But it hurts, it really hurts. It's like swallowing one of Daddy's orange barbecue coals, with it going down your throat and burning your insides, so can we stop? Hugo, really, please, can we stop?' Mathis vomited in a green grove of razor-sharp ferns.

'Okay, everyone, let's stop, okay.' They were forced to stay there for a moment, so that Mathis could vomit again, and Raphael and Lilou collapsed on the ground, taking advantage of the opportunity, holding their stomachs, silent or groaning, at any rate unable to stand up or get a word out. To say what, anyway? *You were right, Hugo? We shouldn't have eaten those berries?* The vomit hurled into the vegetation stunk badly enough to say it for them. And the sight of children writhing on the ground foretold the future that now everyone could predict in looking at them: no one would take another step. They had to take time to recover, or at least wait for it to pass, because nothing else was imaginable in this state. Or else what if they were all to die here, vomiting or starving, poisoned or dying of hunger? But this possibility had to be chased from their minds, nipped in the bud, because what then?

A day had passed like a breeze that caresses no cheek, like the sound of a tree falling in a dead forest, not changing anything in the grand order of things that decides who shall die and who shall be spared. Help would not come, because no one had called for it. None of the children had found the road, because they were all dead or sick or stuck waiting for the sick to die.

And Enzo decided he had to go on.

Sandra, who remained the last adult wandering the woods, was stupidly and blindly walking in circles, her remaining strength being sapped by her stubborn refusal to find a way out of the ordeal, chanting more than calling the names of Fred and her daughter, with no remaining hope of an answer, but instead like the strange, hypnotic reflex that can seize young children, suspended in the incantatory pronunciation of the same words, stripped of their meaning by virtue of being said over and over again out loud. Could she still picture a plausible future where it all worked out, the group was found, Jade saved, everyone back at home in the dry warmth of their day-to-day lives? Maybe not the best of lives, with the odd thing she would like to change: a husband who is more active, a bigger house, a bigger salary to pay for a cleaning lady once or twice a month to save her from some of the drudgery, an average life, but hers, to be sure, one that she truly loved or had at least learned to accept. Was she now able to miss it or even hope to get back to it? What could she be thinking, staggering, filled with the pain of thousands of steps, the memory of which sang out like a choir of martyrs in her thighs and on the soles of her feet? Stunned by her own voice, which was filled more with shame than determination, was she even able to picture her final moments, dying of hunger or fatigue with the brazenly vibrant moss as a backdrop, or was she walking like a robot with no goal, no plan, waiting for some event, hero, or god to save her from her pathetic destiny?

Regardless, Sandra had walked the whole day without realizing that she was being stalked by the most dangerous creature in the forest. Enzo sat down at regular intervals to watch her out of the corner of his eye, nibbling on a granola bar or using the tip of his little knife to whittle a piece of bark that never quite took the shape he wanted. And as always, idiotically punctual, Sandra came back after having gone in a circle she didn't realize was one. Enzo never got tired of it, never considered cutting the absurd ride short by revealing his presence or slitting his prey's throat the way his father did to finish off an injured boar. Strangely calm and uncharacteristically patient, he felt unfamiliar feelings stir as he studied the awkward gait of the mother calling out to her daughter, without the jealousy or rage he normally felt when he considered other people's happy families. He even felt a sort of sad empathy when he heard the roar of a passing truck on the road not far off, which she didn't even notice, continuing her walk in a direction that was necessarily the wrong one because it wasn't even a direction. The woman seemed so kind, so caring. Maybe she could take care of him, even if just for a few hours. Talk to him, comfort him. Stroke his hair if he got tired. That may have been why, at the end of the afternoon, when the sun was already hiding behind the thousands of tree trunks that rose up before him and the light was slowly fading, making Sandra shout a little softer, Enzo decided to get up and approach her.

'Ma'am! Ma'am!'

He had rehearsed the performance a hundred times in his head, going over what he would say and how he would say it, frightened and chilled to the bone, at least in his illusion, miming distress and fatigue, lowering his eyes in solicitude for this woman who should, upon seeing him, feel like a beacon in the night, like smoke rising from the freighter whose course by chance intersects with that of a makeshift raft on the ocean in desperate need of repair.

'Ma'am! Ma'am!' Not saying anything more, just enjoying her tender gaze, that of a mother disappointed, of course, at not having found her own daughter, but pleased to see that the children in the group could be alive somewhere, sheltered, then worried as well and, finally, wondering what happened. Why was Enzo wandering around on his own? Where were the others? Did he run away or did the group split up, with each child fending for himself or herself? And Jade? Where was Jade?

'Where is Jade?' Sandra asked as a reflex, before showing any concern for Enzo's health and how he got there. 'Is she okay?' Enzo opened his big, sad eyes. *So adult*, she thought.

'I don't know, ma'am, yes, maybe, I don't know. I got lost,' Enzo answered, exactly as he imagined his part in the conversation, without saying anything to worry the already worried mother – oh, she had good reason to be – without giving her reason to keep walking, faster, and faster still. Appease her instead, encourage her to sit down and wait for night to fall and then spend it consoling this little boy lost in the woods and in the rest of his life.

'I'm tired, ma'am, so tired,' he repeated, guessing that the growing darkness would end up convincing this woman who had been walking in circles for so long to finally stop for a tangible, human reason, more powerful than just a cowardly retreat in the face of fatigue, pain, and discouragement. But Sandra didn't exactly throw open her arms to the lost child. Her eyes grew veiled as she remembered the disturbing incident from the day before. It wasn't just the fact that he had crushed a snail that was shocking; it was the vicious look in his eye as he did it. *A lunatic*, she had thought at the time. *This child is crazy.* But now that he turned his downcast eyes and beseeching pout to her, she felt forced to reconsider her judgment and soften her hostility. Children were capable of being wicked and sadistic, but they were still children, after all.

'Okay, Enzo, come here,' she finally said. 'It will be okay. I'll get you home. But you have to tell me where the others are. In which direction?'

'I don't know, ma'am,' Enzo answered, wrapping his little arms around her heavy thighs. 'I don't know. I'm lost.'

'How did you get lost?' she insisted. She had to know.

Yes, the child needed comforting. Yes, she was the adult. But she had to know.

'Is everything okay? Is Jade okay? Why didn't Fred answer when I called him?'

'Yes, ma'am,' Enzo answered, allowing a sob to rise in him that – strangely – seemed sincere. 'Everyone is okay. We didn't know where you were. We thought you went home with Hugo's mom. Fred tried to call you.'

Stupid phone, Sandra thought, as Enzo sobbed, letting unfeigned sorrow seep out of him, genuine sadness that had nothing to do with Fred's death or the tragic situation in which he found himself, but rather with the serenity of the current moment. Yes, for maybe the first time in his life, he felt a sort of peace. Here in the middle of the hostile woods, where he was both filled with and surrounded by barbarity, he suddenly felt like he could give in to emotion. With no witnesses, no one to judge, with arms around him holding him tight. Had his mother ever taken the time to do this? To just hold him and console him? He felt like he could forget it all, snuggle up and let someone else take his fate in hand, at least for a few hours, and feel no shame. It was to be expected, after all. He was just a child, wasn't he? But as far back as he could remember, how many times had he ever really been able to behave like a child? How many times had he been able to cry, really bawl, uncontrollably, with a child's sorrow? Maybe once, or twice, until his father would give him something to cry about. 'Are you a man or a mouse?' he would say, or one of the other pat sentences he repeated all the time, which, along with a smack, was his idea of an upbringing.

'And Fred?' Sandra asked, 'Did he call someone else? The forest rangers? The fire department?'

But Enzo couldn't answer. Now he was weeping. Buried in Sandra's fleshy thighs, he was crying like a baby, hiccuping and sniffling. It was so good. It was as if everything disappeared when you cried that hard, as if the tears purified everything, erased everything, stopped time, pulling him into this abandon.

'Enzo, answer me!' Sandra pressed him.

'I don't know, ma'am,' Enzo stammered between sobs. 'I don't know what he did.'

Sandra realized that she would get nothing out of the boy. She was no further ahead than when she found him. The only difference was that now she would have a new burden to shoulder. She had gotten lost in the woods like an idiot. So far, it wasn't all that serious: she alone was suffering the consequences. But now, the slightest choice she made could decide the fate of this frightened child.

'Don't worry. Don't cry. We should rest,' she said, 'and then we'll find the others.'

And astonishingly, Enzo didn't even think of making fun of such an idiotic promise from a woman who had been walking in circles in the woods for hours, and he settled for crying some more in the plump arms of this sad, substitute mother.

The person pretending to be lost but who wasn't and the person pretending not to be lost but who was found a carpet of inland pine needles that would serve as a dry bed and sat down, their backs against the threadbare conifer, huddled against each other, satisfying each other's need for the comfort and safety they had been deprived of the night before and maybe for all nights to come. Sandra pressed Enzo to her breast, put her arms around him to make him feel like something was covering him, like there was a barrier, albeit symbolic, between him and the chill of the night. She had spent hours dreaming of holding her own child in her arms, so her gesture toward him served her as well, like an ersatz tenderness, a simulation of the reunion she could revel in for a few hours while waiting to truly experience this happiness, which suddenly didn't seem so far out of reach. Fred must have called for help. They might even be there before night-fall. Everything seemed possible again. It was possible that she would find Jade. It was possible that they would not die here. This little person, who was drying his tears in her arms, was proof of this, incontrovertible proof, vivid confirmation that managed to prevent her from seeing the brown smears of dried blood in the child's dark hair.

'Can you tell me a story, ma'am?' Enzo asked, pressed against this plump woman and burning with an affection that was brand new to him. 'I can't get to sleep without a story,' he lied, surprising himself at having come up with this strange request, he who despised stories, who hated being told them more than anything, who seethed with rage in listening to edifying tales in which a ridiculous moral turned the entertainment to a gaping wound from which the pus of the lesson seeped, as if no story, no life, no event on earth deserved to be told if it did not contain the inevitable lesson that people revel in and that bore to tears first their children, then their fellow creatures, and finally the unfortunate cohorts of future generations once they develop a taste for writing them.

Enzo's life, and probably yours too, would serve as a lesson for no one. It emerges, endures, and ends without anyone arranging its episodes into a narrative, organizing them so that onlookers can take them in, ideally. Because there are no onlookers, and the lives that go untold are like pebbles thrown up in the air: their linear trajectory does not help people feel better, act better, be more understanding. Their abject monotony even tends to inspire the opposite: violence, madness, and hatred. And that is why no story is ever told that fails to have a lesson, because telling a story without a point destroys civilization a little. And while Enzo didn't realize it, this was why he hated stories, because he hated being told what to do, like his father did, like Fred did, like all adults did and would continue to do until the boy was properly trained, until he stopped once and for all wanting to destroy civilization, little by little, every day, in his own way.

'Once upon a time,' Sandra began, without having the foggiest what she would say next. 'Once upon a time,' she repeated, in the clinging shadows of the evening, while far away, or maybe right nearby, Lilou, Mathis, and Raphael were twisting on the ground, moaning through the gurgling of their incandescent white vomit, their bodies under assault, trying to expel the poison through any means possible, not realizing that it was too late and that the retching, fever, and spasms would only make the suffering of little bodies that were already suffering too much to bear. Hugo held Raphael's hand and Jade held Lilou's, and no one was holding Mathis's because he was already unconscious, his head resting in a puddle of excrement streaked with green and red, mixed in with the dead leaves and needles, his hair wet with sweat and bile, sweeping the black soil to the rhythm of his convulsions as he lay dying. Hugo and Jade occasionally looked at each other in silence, gnawed at by hunger, but happy to be enjoying that privilege, miraculous survivors damned to witness the punishment of those who would not survive. It went on for so long, the cries, the groans, the terror, the silent calls for help from the three sick children, that the heavy looks they exchanged tended to show only the horror, gratitude, and distress that also awoke in them the shameful wish that it all be over soon, that they be able to let go of the chilled, damp hands and return to having both feet firmly planted in the land of the living. Let them die – no, don't let them die, but let them stop suffering and sleep, rest for the night by their side, let the cries peter out, so that they can once again be afraid of the murmurs of the forest, find a hollow trunk, perhaps, and huddle up against one another like last night, which was so pleasant and peaceful in retrospect, despite the worry about possibly being lost and the fear of discovery by Enzo. It was so peaceful because at the time they thought, supposed, or sensed that it was impossible to go through anything worse than what they were going through.

Worse, Sandra thought, *yes, much worse if I can't find another story to tell than the horrors going through my head. Hop-o'-My-Thumb is abandoned by his parents, Hansel, Gretel, and dopey Snow White meet a witch, there are ogres, wolves, evil spells: how could a child lost in the forest sleep after hearing that?*

'Once upon a time,' Sandra repeated again, this time deciding to improvise, 'there was a little boy named Eliott. Eliott was like other little boys; he got good grades at school, he didn't make waves, and he didn't tease his little classmates, but Eliott had a problem: he never spoke. When he was younger, his parents had worried, and thought he was slow or unable to speak, and they visited every doctor they could find. They all agreed: Eliott wasn't mute or stupid; if Eliott wasn't talking, it was because he didn't want to.'

And the three little children, twisting on the ground, didn't want to die, here, in their vomit, but that was what was happening. But you need to understand, and not be scared, because a child doesn't die like you, an adult or an old person reading these lines. Children die without having had a chance to picture the end, without a sense of it being born and maturing within them. They die the same way they get lice or a skinned knee. They die without understanding, with their childish naïveté imagining death the way they imagine April showers, meteorological inevitabilities that eventually pass, not knowing or realizing that this inevitability does not pass. Three little children crumpled on the sticky ground dazed by new pain. *Is it possible to suffer this much?* their eyes said. *You mean the life I have ahead contains this type of pain? If I survive, will this ordeal repeat?* It was a stream of questions, a spring flowing from their wet eyelashes and tasting of their purple lips, a bilious torrent that spewed forth and landed at the feet of their helpless classmates, Hugo and Jade, who were stunned by the latest spectacle, each holding the hand of someone who is leaving, and then, suddenly, without real-izing it, holding the hand of someone else who will make it, Hugo and Jade, fingers touching and palms pressed together, two delicate witnesses of the brutal obliteration of their friends. In their position, a normal person would have been gripped by the same alarm, a person who was not Enzo, perhaps all of humanity except Enzo, staking out the very definition, I'm sure you would agree, of what is human and what is not, of what lies naked in all its savagery.

'And then one day,' Sandra continued, 'one day when Eliott was walking along the long, grey canal that ran behind his house, one day Eliott, little Eliott, heard what sounded like a cry. So he walked faster, looked into the distance, and in the dirty water of the canal saw a stir and the thrashing limbs of a child. Yes, it looked like a child, a child who was struggling, waving, screaming in the froth his own terror produced.'

How can I be saying this? Sandra wondered. *How can I tell such a horrible story to a child at night in the middle of the woods? There has to be a happy ending, she told herself again, I have to find an ending that is so wonderful and happy that he will forget the evening shadows and the whispers of the night. No problem. I know what to say. It's not so hard to invent stories with happy endings, after all. If we ever escape this infernal night and this inextricable forest, I may take this up seriously, write stories and tell them to children. It would help pass the time. It would relieve the boredom, if we ever get out of here.*

'But for that,' she went on, 'little Eliott needed to talk, shout, call out for help, for someone, anyone who could come to the aid of the child who was drowning before his very eyes.'

And similarly the three children were dying in front of them, retching with nothing left in them but the horror of still being alive, and suddenly Sandra squinted at the dashed dream of one day being a storyteller for good little girls and boys, because it was moist, and warm, and unexpected, the thing that was dripping down her chest, and close by the little reedy voice said, 'Your story sucks,' and Raphael bid a guttural goodbye to what remained of his memories, and Jade noticed with astonishment that she had tears left to spill over the body of Lilou, and back to Sandra seeing the shadow of the little Enzo rise up before her, still clutching in his hand the bloody knife that he had just planted in her throat.

'You can't,' Sandra said, shaken by her inability to understand. 'You won't hear the end of the story.'

Her final word, 'story,' was swallowed up in the gurgle of the blood spurting from her severed carotid artery. *It cuts well*, Enzo thought. *It slices through meat.* 'What good is an unfinished story?' Sandra tried to say, instead making a comical gurgle that, even to her, made no sense at all. What was there to say or think now that it was becoming clear that it would be the last thing she would ever say or think? Send her love to her husband? And what would he do with it? No, Jade. She's the one who deserves to be the focus of the last seconds of her existence. Think of Jade and send her all the love she could imagine. But she didn't manage it. And as she died, what Sandra had in mind was the terrible suspense she had created: would little Eliott call for help? Would he make a sound for the first time in his life and save the child, who, without him, would sink to the bottom of the canal and into the night that is waiting to fall on every one of us? How ridiculous. How sad that her last moments should be wasted on the fate of an imaginary child, a ghost she had conjured, caught in the web of her own fiction. *I could have thought of my daughter while dying*, she thought, *but instead I'm thinking about some little ninny I invented.* And to see whether the flesh in other parts of the body was as tender, Enzo purposefully plunged his knife under Sandra's shoulder, then again in her thigh, then where he thought her stomach was, and so on, like a methodical scientist, in a number of other places on her body to determine the degree of resistance, and with no regard, of course, for the fact that Sandra, having lost most of her blood inside and out, had been dead for several minutes before he finally tired of the experiment. Hugo and Jade were a few hundred metres, perhaps eleven kilometres, in any case a few centuries away, closer to each other than they ever had been or ever would be again, hands inextricably joined, curled up, spooning, entwined like lovers who don't love each other but who love being alive, together, at the same time, because that is enough to give them the strength to stay huddled up, holding tight, while those around them are in their death throes, dying in the loneliness of the night, Raphael and Lilou and Mathis, alive yesterday, they remembered, and today no more, talking and crying a moment ago and now nothing, no crying, no moaning, no heat, or just a little, now waning, so cold, abnormally cold, and not moving, incredibly, supernaturally. *Have we ever seen*, they thought, *such complete immobility? Even our stuffed animals have more life in their faces and their eyes than the three twisted, ashen friends, lying among the dried needles of the undergrowth. How can we, and how, if we indeed can, be so still, when we are or have been alive? Objects now, not currently animated by breath. Children still warm. Is that what is in store for us? All of us one day, or just us, soon? Showing signs of life for how much longer? How long can we last, eating wind and drinking our own pleas?* Enzo removed his knife from Sandra's split eyeball and reached his fingers toward it to spread open the wound. Was there something glimmering at the back? When the end came, did people's eyes for a while keep a faint trace of what they had last seen? Did a few points of that light settle at the back of the dead person's eyes, slowly going out, like the ember of a fire that is no longer being fed? If that were the case, Enzo didn't see anything and found only pulp and blood as he searched the eyeball, dirty muck and disappointment at yet again giving up part of the magic he had been promised.

'Are they dead?' Jade asked her friend, her chin resting against his shoulder blade, unable to cry or react in any way whatsoever to the question she had asked automatically, not worrying about or even wanting to know the answer.

'I don't know,' said Hugo, who was smart and knew lots of things, who was sometimes at the head of the class, when it wasn't Lucas, but who was also a child, a small child. 'You are a big boy now,' his grandmother said when he went into Grade 1. 'You're a big boy.' *No, I'm not, I'm not, I'm a kid, a little kid, you get it? I'm not a doctor. I'm not a teacher. I'm tired. And hungry. So I don't know. Maybe they're dead. Maybe not. I'm scared too. I want to go to sleep in my bed, with my teddy bears, and my mommy, and I want to leave this place and never set foot in the forest again.* And already on their knees, the huddled children lay down now that night had well and truly fallen. They pressed up against their classmates, as if to comfort them, console them for being dead, or maybe to help usher them into the next world, not knowing whether the next world exists, absently holding their hands until deciding they were too cold, clutching at their clothes like benevolent security blankets as they slipped into sleep, five little bodies hunched in the chilly north wind of the night, five little figures about whom it is now hard to know which were alive and which were dead, equally still, similarly broken, lost, alone, desperate, and just as helpless.

Hugo's sleep was deep and uninterrupted, undisturbed by cold, hunger, or dampness, because his body was still growing, a long way from being done, and it had reached the limit of its ability to expend energy it didn't have. Sleep brought on by starvation and extreme fatigue is like a rotten board drifting on a calm ocean, at times undeniably floating, but occasionally dipping below the surface long enough that onlookers would be forgiven for thinking all was lost and that the board had sunk for good. Hugo's sleep swung similarly between deep drowsiness and something worse, a kind of unconsciousness you don't necessarily come back from but that he invariably came back from, driven by a mysterious force, a physiological refusal to let go, which had previously been mental. Was it the powerful bond with his mother that kept bringing him back to this side of the line? Or the duty to save Jade, the last victim he could help, as he was unconsciously inhabited by the feeling that he had developed from living fatherless in a world that tries to drive home the idea that men protect women and that women need protection? Whatever the reason, through this second brutish night, he stayed alive enough to open his eyes yet again in the morning and be greeted by the pinch of a night spent hungry. It was early, because thick mist was still caught in the trees and hovered, as if stuck, right above the ground. Once he realized where he was and why, Hugo, still lying on his side, let escape a heart-rending sob, even more painful because it was uncontrollable, a rogue wave that emerged from the depths of the ocean and the tables of probability, engulfing the small, rotten board. He cried, shouted, called for his mommy, clawing at the ground with his remaining strength, then suddenly stopped as if he had heard something. Hugo vigorously rubbed his eyes to dispel the tears and make it easier to see, and he sat up to survey his surroundings. What immediately struck him was not a noise but the absence of noise. Absence of noise, absence of body – in the dawn that turned everything grey, Hugo had just realized that Jade had disappeared. Three bodies on the ground – their sallowness, their stillness, the armies of insects that were climbing all over them and crawling in and out of their orifices confirmed that they were no longer children. But Jade wasn't among them, neither dead nor alive.

'Jade!' Hugo called out. 'Jade, where are you?'

At the back of his throat, he had the vivid memory of the sob he wanted to contain. No answer, of course. Why would there have been one? Jade would never have left him of her own free will, even to pee, even for a few minutes. Hugo was little, but this was something he knew, and if Jade was no longer within earshot, it was because there was a problem.

'Jade,' Hugo called out again, 'are you there?' He wasn't really expecting an answer and yet one came.

'I think Jade had a little accident,' Enzo's jovial voice said, somewhere, faint, far from where the sun would finish rising. And something collapsed inside Hugo. Sobs rose once more, but this time they contained enough acid to dissolve him completely. Was there nothing left in this world that was worth opening your eyes in the morning and fighting for? Would the bad guys always win? Are our efforts to live in peace simply doomed to failure? Will the bad guys always be bad guys? Will the good guys spend their whole lives taking punches and throwing rocks into the water with all of their might and getting nothing more in return than a ridiculous *sploosh* and the shame of failure? *And what about me*, Hugo thought for a fraction of a second of despondency. *Will I have to spend my life trying to convince dogs not to devour puppies? What do I have to do? How do I have to do it? Will I always have to think? Or sometimes, just sometimes, will I be allowed to run straight at the enemy, toward the source of my torment, and take him out, massacre him, beat him to a pulp, like he did to my teacher? Will I have the right to do that one day? Do I have the right to do it now?* And, dragging himself enraged from the pile of scree he had become, Hugo swallowed the mucus that was caught at the back of his throat, lifted his head toward the source of his terror, and his hate, and his incomprehension, and his fatigue, and of everything that had put him here, starving and weak and exhausted and miserable and in shock, alone now in the middle of a hostile forest, gathering what may have been his last bit of strength before foundering like a rotten plank to the bottom of the ocean. He darted east, in Enzo's direction, to do battle, to die, to win, no matter the outcome of this absurd confrontation, but so that this would end, with no thought, no plan, no strategy, so that everything would end with killing while being killed or vice versa. Hugo ran, brushing against the tree trunks, at times feeling his legs slip out from under him, straight ahead, following the evil voice that cut like a merciless blade planted in his marrow and twisting, to make it more painful. 'So, did you find your girlfriend?' Enzo said, or maybe he didn't, what with the voices and the chirping of the birds and the creaking of wood, all the sounds of the forest drowned out by the wind that rushed into his ears in that mad dash, straight on, toward the voice, toward the east, toward the resolution, he thought, he felt in his bones, of all this horror, this horror. And he ran even faster without looking at, or doing whatever he could not to look at, but not quite managing it, Jade's broken body, crumpled against a tree, left there like one would leave a piece of clothing that had become too hot or too heavy, a cheap piece of clothing, at any rate, for which one had not had the time to develop the slightest affection. Her arms were folded in a way that seemed impossible, legs beneath her, or maybe to the side, forming an angle that no anatomy could endure, and finally the head, the face, open in several places like a thick book that was read and then left there, nearby, until the reader could get back to it. Even running as fast as he could, the eyes, pierced, weeping black blood, he couldn't help but see the eyes and think, *What? Why do that to her? What had she ever done to him? What did any of us ever do to him? Why keep going and do all this harm and not spare anyone?* Why? He would have to stop. Someone would have to stop him.

Hugo slowed his running once he recognized where he was. The camp wasn't so far away after all, he thought, when he came upon the line of little tents in the sunlight, the logs around the fire now extinguished, and the macabre and curiously less colourful scene than the one that was burned in his memory. Fred's body didn't seem to have moved, the objects and the clothes the children had abandoned in their panic were still lying scattered awaiting their owners, and not far away, the emptied backpacks, their contents spread out on the ground, indicated that Enzo had made do with taking a little food and drink from the children's luggage, with no concern for disguising or concealing his crime. Hugo's stomach rumbled as the image of cookies hit him, the little cookies he didn't really like but that were the only thing his mother would let him eat for his after-school snack. Now he dreamed of them. Swaying as if drunk from fatigue, he wondered whether he could catch his breath and sit down for just a minute, rifle through his backpack, take out the little cookies and devour them, whether he had time to do that before heading off in pursuit of Enzo again. It was worth a try. So, panting, Hugo headed toward the colourful bags, but even before reaching them he could tell that they hadn't just been emptied: they had been partially devoured. Amid the torn fabric and shredded plastic wrappers, there seemed to be not one crumb of food left. To be sure, Hugo bent over the remains of his bag, just as the voice rang out again.

'You won't find anything,' Enzo said. 'I ate a lot of it, and the animals came in the night to help themselves. Foxes or boars. They didn't leave anything. They even ate what was in the shed.'

Hugo plopped down on the ground, perhaps out of aggravation or simply because he didn't have the strength to keep his balance, then he turned his head toward the voice, expecting to see nothing, just the cold ashes of the campfire, Fred's dried blood, and the lonely silhouettes of the trees all around him. But Enzo was there, standing on the tallest of logs, smiling, triumphant, clearly in fine form, his arms slowly swinging the length of his body, one of them made longer by the flash of a wet, dirty knife.

'The light,' he went on, 'doesn't stay in their eyes.'

He paused, lifted his head to the white sky, then dropped it toward the knife.

'Or else I didn't see it,' he said, as if bored.

Hugo smelled the sweat running down his temples and under his arms, soaking his pyjamas as if he had wet himself, and now, in addition to his fatigue, his hunger, and his fear, there was a warm, private shame, the unpleasant memory of the gloomy nights when he would wake up crying, still half-asleep, in the macabre glow of the moon while he waited for his mother to quickly change the sheets, and even though she never grumbled about his accidents, the shame clung to him all the same, of having done something wrong, even without meaning to. That was the worst: not being enough, not being the big boy he would have liked to have become faster, imagining his mother wanted him to be that big boy even faster.

'You're mean,' Hugo said, an obvious fact that needed stating – maybe it had never been stated. Maybe Enzo didn't know that what he was doing was wrong – one could always hope – and maybe these two words would make him see sense. Perhaps it was so obvious – 'what you are doing is wrong,' 'killing people is wrong' – that no one had ever thought to point it out. But did Hugo really want to? Did he want Enzo to put his head in his hands and cry in remorse? No. Definitely not. It was too late now, and the only thing that would release this tension was physical confrontation, with as much fury as possible, with vengeance, with all the brutality needed to ease it. Regrets? Apologies? Mashing his little face into the ground probably wouldn't be enough to forgive what he had put them through in recent hours, the horrors he had committed, the people he had dispatched, so no, Hugo wouldn't take any more; he would kill or be killed, to the extent that a six-year-old can under-stand what that means.

'You killed my friends,' Hugo said panting, seething with what was left of his rage.

Enzo took a moment to search for a good comeback, a sarcastic retort to his classmate's pathetic anguish, but didn't find it and settled for bursting into a forced laugh, the limited conviction of which stopped it from breaking through the curtain of trees around them. For Hugo, perhaps this closeness, this one-sided show of triumph, was intolerable. He had already planned to kill him, or to try with all his might, but to endure this laughter that was directed at him – not at the cuckoos, not at the rabbits, not at the grass snakes in the woods, but at him alone – put the final touches on the black rage swelling within him and gave him the energy to stand up, foaming at the mouth, on legs wracked with fatigue. He shot Enzo a look devoid of empa-thy or even an ounce of compassion, a look of pure hate and vengeance, and he ran as fast as he could, ran, and yelled, a cry that was so solemn but that could be either the first or the last, as weak as the first, shrill and irrepressible, necessarily a bit ridiculous but primal, indisputably, one of those impulses that no one would be brave enough to mock, because sometimes despite their clumsiness and their awkwardness, despite everything, they could be fatal. So Hugo ran, like a bull, like a bison, like a buffalo, like a thing that charges, and, yelling all that was left inside, flying like a crossbow straight at Enzo's heart, straight toward where it should have been found, in his sworn enemy's chest, which was puffed out with pride. Faced with the surprising violence and the desperate quality of the act, which was somehow ridiculously in vain, Enzo didn't flinch or move an inch. *He'll hit me and then what?* he thought, laughing even harder. *He wants us to fall over. He wants us to roll around on the ground like we're having fun, like a sport, like we're blowing off steam and killing time. So yes, why not, let's fight, Hugo, like we did with the other kids, in the schoolyard, not really hitting or intending to hurt anyone. Hit me and wait for me to hit you back; let there be no consequences, as is appropriate to the children we are, so that we can stop being responsible for anything serious. Come on. I would love to play a little for a few more minutes.* This was how, weak and innocuous though he was, Hugo managed to barrel into Enzo at full force, shoulder projecting into his ribs, pushing like a rugby player with all of his meagre strength, lifting his target a few centimetres off the stump where he was perched, still beaming, then pushing with his arms whose bones even seemed limp, pushing like you hit when you're not used to doing it or don't really want to do it, pushing straight ahead in a gesture that may have been harmless, but that conveyed enough intention to get the message across. What with the shock and the shove, Enzo lost his balance and, not managing to grab hold of his attacker's pyjamas or limbs, sailed smoothly in reverse from the stump to the ground, a curved trajectory through the cool morning air, which surprised even its initiator, who was ready to do battle after the initial collision and who suddenly found himself deprived of his target, Enzo, who was not moving, a few metres away, his head landing with a horrible crack against another stump, where a few hours earlier one of his hapless victims probably sat.

There was blood, a body lying motionless, and big, dead eyes staring at the overcast sky; for a moment Hugo thought that was it, he had killed him, that everything would finally end, here and now. But Enzo moved, his eyelashes fluttered, he lifted his head slightly, tried to smile but couldn't quite manage. His eyes spun one last time, and he went limp, plunging into what appeared to be unconsciousness rather than death.

I knocked him out; he's just knocked out, Hugo thought. *It's not over*, he repeated like a lunatic, and then it was all too much, and he screamed, not articulating anything, no call for help, no victory cry, no invective; he just let everything he had held in up to this point come out, because there were the others, the onlookers in his mind, watching him and waiting and judging him and expecting the best. Because that was the role he had played for his classmates, for the rest of the world, for the world of classmates you can reign over peacefully, whether you are magnanimous like him or a tyrant like Enzo, but whose scrutiny you always feel, an expectation that weighs on you, that you forget but that clings to your back and your chest like a tight suit that you constantly feel and yet don't feel. So when Enzo collapsed, unconscious, suddenly that weight lifted, because for the first time since the beginning of this horror story, he was alone, truly alone, without his mother, who was far away, without his friends, who were dead, without his lifelong nemesis, who, from where he lay, no longer had the luxury of making fun of him. His scream carried all of his weariness, as the sun was going down on the world.

Hugo swayed and almost fell too, as he turned to take in his surroundings. *I won't kill him*, he thought, *but I have to stop him from doing anything else. The police have to come and arrest him and lock him up forever.*

The camp was in disarray: a body, a pool of dried blood, an unconscious child, the ground littered with debris from backpacks, clothing, and plastic food wrappers.

Hugo staggered to the scattered bags and from a gutted backpack grabbed a web of straps that was virtually intact. The only knots he knew how to tie were for his shoes, but the straps seemed perfect for immobilizing Enzo for good. A few undaunted sunbeams managed to break through the forest's thick curtain of green, but it was still early morning as Hugo pulled on the straps with all his might to secure his classmate to a metal stake firmly stuck in the ground, probably with a concrete base, that was used as an anchor for the camp's seasonal structures: tents, shelters, and clotheslines. Around his back, wrists, and crossed ankles, Hugo tied as many straps, tethers, ropes, and wires as he could find, unsure

{ 136 }

of his ability to create sufficiently solid knots to prevent Enzo from hurting anyone ever again. When he was done – not because he was sure that his structure would hold, but because there were no straps left – he struggled to stand on trembling legs that barely supported him, and without thinking, headed for the burned-out campfire where Fred's body was lying.

'One-one-two' he repeated in his head, 'if I have a big problem when Mommy isn't here, I have to call 112.' He paused before the terrible spectacle of blood, flesh, and flies, which he saw for the first time up close and in the light of day, and despite his disgust and the suffocating smell of rot, he shoved his hands into the pockets of Fred's pants in search of his phone.

Nothing. His phone was gone. Or had he put it somewhere else? Hugo didn't have the strength to look. He struggled to stand again, rocking for a moment like an off-kilter pendulum, tried to figure out which direction he should head in, thought about the dirt road they had come down when he and Fred and his mom and his friends arrived, an eternity ago. That way, yes, it had to be that way. All of the dirt roads looked alike, particularly since black spots had started to appear intermittently in his blurred vision, due to the lack of food, water, sleep, and warmth. He set off, slowly, with determination, a small animal barely dressed, not well armed against the brutality of the forest, but still strong enough to be alive and to hope to remain that way until he reached the road and could stick out his thumb or wave his hand and stop a passerby, a car or a truck or whatever vehicle he could find, provided it would take him home, to be with his mother. Not to the hospital but home, to his bedroom with all of his toys that told his own private story, the only story he had known until now. Get to the road, raise his arm, wave his hand, and collapse onto the car seat, and not have to think anymore, not have to be afraid of anything, not Enzo, not wild animals, not poisonous mushrooms, or any of the other horrors that lie in wait in the shadows for children. Raise his arm, way up high, wave his hand, and not have to think anymore. *How will I eat? Where will I sleep? Have I already come this way? Raise my arm, wave my hand like this, and collapse, like this, in the ditch, maybe a little too soon, roll down the slope, barely aware of what is happening, disappear in a tangle of ferns, brambles, and tall grass, my little green pyjamas stained with brown mud and brown blood, the perfect camouflage, not yet dead, not yet unconscious either, but unable to do anything to extricate myself from the bush and my immobility, awake, eyes open, but tired, so tired, looking without seeing a few centimetres from me a placid, gigantic, terrifying stag beetle, unable to do anything, or dream, just dream, roam, wander away and return how many times? With my eyes make night fall and dawn break again, not knowing whether night is falling or my eyelids are growing weaker. Is it night? Is it evening? Has an entire day gone by? Or have the black spots in front of my eyes expanded and draped the world in a funeral veil? My eyes are open, I think they are, open and staring at the fabled insect – Fred would have been so proud of me if he knew I had found one. Fred, can you hear me? I found a stag beetle! Should I believe my eyes – did I fall asleep? Am I still sleeping? Turning his oversized mandibles into dancing swords for my final, furious duel with the beast. You know, the beast, the child-insect with the indestructible carapace, with no fear and no feeling, the monster, a real one, whose hand doesn't* hesitate when it strikes. The one who must be stopped before he does any more harm, the child-insect, who loves nothing and no one, against me, engaging in battle, fists hammering amid bestial screams, animal growls, strangely real, strangely close, right behind me, from the direction I came from, from the direction of the camp, crazed screaming and guttural growls. Am I dreaming or is it real? It sounds like Enzo's voice, Enzo's terrified screams, Enzo's unbearable pain that for a few seconds brings me back to this side of the boundary between the living and those who would rather not be. It's so dark. The day must be done. Night must have fallen. And that voice, the screaming, the distress, the surprising distress from such a demon, the author and architect of so much pain. How can I feel sorry for him? How can I feel the slightest pity for him as he seems to be going through such an ordeal? Yet I want to get up, run to the camp to help him, because his screams, how do I stay indifferent to his screams? How can I delight in them? How can I not want them to stop? Even the killer of every-one I know, of my friends and my teacher, who would have killed me without batting an eye if I hadn't tied him up, even he doesn't deserve this suffering, which sounds like the worst thing a human can endure. Even he who deserves to die, who deserves to be killed, doesn't deserve to be killed like that.

The stag beetle's carapace split open, revealing a pair of translucent amber wings that hummed as they flapped, much slower than the noise suggested. The animal then took to the air and flew out of Hugo's sight. That had happened a few hours ago, long before the screaming. Now all he was aware of was the unmoving stems of the ferns, the hillocks of moss, and, in the air, as if coming from all around him, the screaming, the horrible screaming.

The wild boar had spent the day sleeping in his wallow. He hadn't noticed that all around him children were dying. Then, at the end of the afternoon, he rolled around some more and stretched until he found his legs and was fully awake, then started to trot as he dragged his snout along the ground in search of food. In the early evening hours, his keen sense of smell led him to the edge of the camp, where the night before he and his fellow creatures had eaten so well. He methodically toured the area where the shredded bags formed a multicoloured mosaic on the black soil, but, finding nothing, the beast who had eaten too much yesterday and who was famished today decided to look for another source of sustenance. Over that way, it smelled like cereal, sugar, and chocolate. His snout first came to rest on the fabric of Enzo's Bermuda shorts, the smell of chocolate bars still emanating from the pockets, and, rubbing his head against the shorts, had managed to raise them enough to expose the thigh, the skin, and the flesh, which he bit into without a second thought.

Enzo was so badly hurt, his skull cracked open on the log, plunged by trauma into a state that was not exactly unconsciousness but not wakefulness either, that he didn't even understand that this searing pain that gripped his thigh came from the repeated bites of an animal that was devouring him.

Snorting and snuffling, the boar went at the tender muscle, its appetite whetted by the delicate taste of this strange carrion, juicy, quivering, which seemed even to move at times, trembling under the bites, then, carried away by its gluttony, it rooted around, pulled, bit through the flesh down to the bone. All of this is abstract, we are aware, and maybe you are having a hard time picturing the terror and pain that Enzo felt as the boar started to bite into the flesh of his arm. So we will try to be as precise as possible, so that you can more clearly picture the scene that follows, so that you can fully experience what it would mean to be immobilized, tied up, powerless, suffering, and unable to do anything about it, not even understand it, just suffer and scream intermittently, from pain, of course, but also from terror, when you emerge from this semi-consciousness and find yourself assailed by the stink and the power of an animal four times your weight. Even near comatose, eyes closed, cut off from the world, still you suffer. Did you realize? Can you imagine? You are securely bound. You don't even have the strength to open your eyes. You hear the beast snorting. On top of the pain from the gaping wound on your thigh, there is the pain of your skin, which will soon split open, in another spot, a bit lower, near your knee. You feel the massive beast straddle you, its hooves sink into your belly, its hindquarters and tail strike your face as if you weren't even there, and then its fangs sink into you again. Your nerves light up your entire body as the flesh is ripped from it. You feel the next bite, and the one after that, and you are not even conscious enough to wish that it be the last. You are just suffering, pure, pristine suffering, like hell, the very definition of hell, and worse than death is the certainty that it isn't done with you yet.

You spend the whole day floating in a murky, dark existence, a bad dream that won't stop, and as the minutes pass you plunge into a bottomless abyss; how you would like to touch bottom and know that you have arrived at the terrible pinnacle of your suffering, and how you miss the day that has just ended, unpleasant though it was, but during which no spear pierced you, no fire burned you, when you were floating in this thick torpor, like the delirium brought on by a bad flu, when you had nothing more to do than wait for everything to fade. But since he found you, nothing will fade, and you scream again as the boar shreds your arm, sinks its fangs into your biceps, and inadvertently dislocates your shoulder by tugging on it. The animal gets agitated, growling as it tries to detach what it has in its mouth and starts tossing its heavy head frenetically like a dog shaking, and your arm is still attached to the rest of your body, but the violent movements rip eruptions from you that punctuate the pain that grips you. You thrash in a cage of suffering, your face contorts into hideous grimaces as if you were dreaming of some horror, but you aren't dreaming, the nightmare is right here, in the agony of your stubborn body that refuses to give up. You poor thing. You cling to life, to the image of your arm that will not be carried off in the mouth of the boar working furiously at it. Your leg is bleeding, but not enough to kill you, two jagged, gaping holes that reveal bright white bone, your femur intact, and while the boar gives up on taking your whole arm, which was too solidly tied up by Hugo, you groan again, then moan, then again scream yourself hoarse as the animal settles for ripping off small pieces of meat from your dangling arm.

This is not a moment. There is no time in what you are going through. Your suffering is a place, and you don't know whether you can ever leave this place. You don't even have enough hope to wish that it be over faster. Faster doesn't exist, any more than time itself. You are not alive enough to measure it. You live in a present of incessant pain. It envelops you like a piece of clothing that is too warm, that drowsiness prevents you from removing, in which you sweat, assaulted by nightmarish waves of heat, without the strength to imagine that it would all stop if the boar would decide to go for your head or sever one of your arteries. But no. None of that happens, and the more the grunting boar tears at your flesh, the more you become aware of your condition, the wounded leg you will never get back, the dislocated arm still solidly tied, and the screaming, your screaming, piercing, primal screams you now hear in addition to producing them, screams that agitate the beast, which grunts, spits, striking your mouth with its snout, your noisy, noisy mouth, wanting to shut you up because carrion doesn't scream. It rubs its monstrous teeth against yours to silence you for good. Do you get it? Stay dead. That is what the animal is commanding you to do as it pushes with all of its weight and puts its big black hoof on your torso to bump you with its snout dripping with drool and blood. Maybe that's when you open your eyes, open them wide, once again becoming aware of this mythical, wild beast of the forest your father so often told you was more deadly than a viper. Black fur in your eyes, on your cheek, hot, fetid breath, filled with animal spittle and snot, you become aware again of what is happening to you, but will soon forget and have to relive the same horrified surprise when the next bite awakens you again. You scream in fright and in so many other things, and the boar's black eye stares at you. Suddenly, like an echo, it growls and its cry becomes indistinguishable from your own. The boar gets agitated; it strikes you with its head and hooves, to shut you up, and because that terrifies you even more and you scream even louder, it lunges at your face and bites your mouth. You choke and heave as the boar rubs its snout and tongue on your open mouth, licks you, maybe swallows the blood dripping from your mouth, its tusks like faded daggers threatening to sink into your neck – if they did, your suffering would stop – taking a huge mouthful of you, trying to rip off your cheek, cheekbone, and part of your upper lip, its incisors not sharp enough to sever your flesh, just pinching it hard, painfully, sunk into your face, and then pulling, biting, and tugging at your elastic skin. Can you scream when half of your face has been ripped from your skull? You find out that yes, you can, that the martyr's scream doesn't require a face, maybe not even a body. The scream is just a breath, it's the wind that roars with no throat and whistles with no tongue, and you scream, and you suffer. You dip deeper into the horror of your persistence here on earth. The boar finishes pulling at your face and rips it off. It chews and swallows it, snorting. You think you will pass out, but you are not unconscious yet. You endure. Did your father ever tell you that pigs eat everything: fruits and berries, worms and hare carcasses, that their jaws are powerful enough to grind bones like barley sugar candies? Hadn't you gotten used to seeing him come back from the hunt with one of these beasts in the trunk, unmoving, still warm? Despite his warnings, the large grey-and-black bodies had long stopped scaring you, and you would run your hand over the bristles. You found them too rough, and now, ironically, you will soon lose that very hand, because the pig has just started on it, having finished devouring your face. You feel the snout snatch your closed fist whole, the contact of the rough tongue on your fingertips, and the pressure of teeth on your restrained fist. Then the snout snaps shut, bites, and pulls so hard and so violently that your joint immediately gives way; your hand disappears, and the boar chews it, crushes your fingers, and grinds your bones, soon swallowing it all. Not enough meat, its animal brain must have thought: but how could a child's hand be meaty? The child that you are, with enough pieces remaining to still be considered a child, but for how much longer? What proportion of child pieces barely hanging together is required to still be considered a child? You shriek again, in a moment in time, that is not really time but rather space for infinite suffering, your thigh, your arm, your face, your hand, a sea of blood that you can't even drown in. Everything starts reeling again. The defence mechanisms of a dying body are set in motion. Molecules are produced somewhere inside you to dull the senses and project you onto another plane, but they collide with the nerve impulses that electrify the tiniest remaining piece of flesh and call for reinforcements, conspire against you so you don't pass out or take off running from this danger that is eating you. You thrash. You tremble. You are seized by frantic starts, you try to escape, not knowing that it is all in vain. And in your microscopic inner landscape, a chemical war is being waged, the outcome of which will decide whether or not you are aware of your pain until your final breath. Irritated or disgruntled by your agitation, the boar steps back. You don't know whether this is a good sign. You can't imagine the past or the future. You don't know whether it would be better for the animal to finish what it has started or to leave you like this. You see only its black-and-grey coat, the voracious shadow retreating, and then the urge to cry rises within you. How long has it been since you have done that, to sob and call for your mommy, having long thought you were too big for such a thing? If your father could hear you, he would smack you and call you a sissy. You aren't sure what liquid is running down your face. It might not be tears, you could tell your father to appease his anger.

The boar approaches the campfire, you hear it snort and snuffle when it reaches Fred's body. Without conviction, it shoves it with its snout, sending a cloud of flies into the air. It rummages around, looking for a hunk it can swallow. You can barely hear the sound of its chewing over the sound of your groaning. You feel yourself letting go. The world around you grows dim. Maybe this is when you will fade away for good and join the others who have long been sleeping. But the boar is still hungry. And Fred doesn't seem to be to his taste: too dead, perhaps. It moves away and heads toward you again. The mere sound of its hooves approaching and its ragged breath, which you hear more and more clearly, provoke a spasm of terror in your chest. You don't see the boar – your eyes are swimming in blood and tears – but you smell its musk, the stench of mud, and you know the animal is here. Not moving. Could it be sizing you up? Is it capable of anticipating the feast that awaits? It advances a bit farther and puts two of hooves on your pristine thigh. You feel its hooves with their ragged horn scratch you, and suddenly, striking with its tusks, it rips off your clothes, the pieces of your T-shirt that are not trapped under your bonds, your Bermuda shorts stained with the blood of Jade and her mother, and yours too now. It strips you of everything that is not as tasty, as if arranging a plate before the meal. Who is to say whether you deserve what is happening to you? Whether you were asking for it? Who is to say that cater-pillars deserve to be thrown to the voracious larvae of the potter wasp? The only truth that exists now is that the boar is still hungry, and that there is still something left to eat.

On the flanks, a little on the back, on one calf if you were to look hard enough, inside the skull: these are the places there was something left to eat on Enzo's body when the boar had finished with him. No one could say exactly when he died, nor how much suffering he endured. The alarm was raised too late by the bus driver who, not seeing the children walk up the dirt road as they had agreed, had headed into the woods and discovered just some of the horror. Two terrified police officers established the preliminary facts of the case, soon joined by dozens of colleagues who began combing the woods in search of the children. The scene of the crime – because that's what it appeared to be – stretched over hectares. While a team worked with the families and the school to compile a list of the children, a major investigative effort got underway in the forest to secure the area and perform a methodical search. The phones of the responsible adults were called: Sandra's went to voice mail, where her awkward voice tried to be funny, Nathalie's went to the default operator's message, and Fred's rang in the back pocket of a half skeleton.

Thirty or so police officers walked the dirt road alongside which Hugo had collapsed. Twelve others half-heartedly searched, without seeing, for a body that in that moment might still have been alive. It took dogs, handsome German shepherds with soft black-and-brown fur, for the rescue team to find Hugo, hidden under thick ferns, in the ditch where he fell. But the child had died long before, and, with him, our hope.

Grégoire Courtois lives and works in Burgundy, where he runs the independent bookstore Obliques, which he bought in 2011. A novelist and playwright, he has published three novels with Le Quartanier: *Révolution* (2011), *Suréquipée* (2015), and *Les lois du ciel* (2016). In 2013 he founded Caractères, an international book festival in Auxerre, which he continues to run.

Rhonda Mullins has translated many books into English, including Dominique Fortier's *The Island of Books*, Elise

Turcotte's *Guyana*, Louis Carmain's *Guano*, and Anaïs Barbeau-Lavalette's *Suzanne*, which was a Canada Reads finalist for 2019. Her translation of Jocelyne Saucier's *And the Birds Rained Down* was a contender for the 2015 Canada Reads, and she won the Governor General's Literary Award for Translation for Saucier's *Twenty-One Cardinals*.

Typeset in Oneleigh, a playful and expressive face designed by Nick Shinn in 1999. Oneleigh has obvious roots in traditional roman serifed types, however this face takes on an eccentric character of its own due to its unique forms and loose, almost hand-drawn appearance in both display and text settings, making it very lively on the page.

Printed at the Coach House on bpNichol Lane in Toronto, Ontario, on Rolland paper. This book was printed with vegetable-based ink on a 1973 Heidelberg KORD offset litho press. Its pages were folded on a Baum-folder, gathered by hand, bound on a Sulby Auto-Minabinda, and trimmed on a Polar single-knife cutter.

Edited by Alana Wilcox
Designed by Crystal Sikma
Cover design by Ingrid Paulson
Cover art 'Forest scene summer' by Currier & Ives, Library of Congress
Author photo by Justine Latour © Le Quartanier
Translator photo by Owen Egan

Coach House Books
80 bpNichol Lane
Toronto, ON M5S 3J4
Canada

416 979 2217
800 367 6360

mail@chbooks.com
www.chbooks.com